Bad Creek

a novel

~

Kenneth P. Smith

PHENIX BOOKS

Middleton House Publishing, Ltd, Co.
Greenville, South Carolina

To Mary

PROLOGUE

It is raining and has been for three days, a cold steady drizzle leaking from a low sky the color of lead. A brown dog lies forlornly on the damp concrete of one of the stoops, barely out of the rain, but staring out at it, moving only occasionally to scratch behind its ear with a hind paw. The low, brick buildings of the project are dull, reddish brown, and wet. They seem huddled together like cattle in a pasture, miserable and unsheltered from the relentless wetness, but mindless of it. Except for the dog, nothing moves. No one comes or leaves. The dingy windows of the apartments look out over the asphalt yard like blank, pupil-less eyes. Litter is strewn about, but it is glued to the earth by the rain. A high chain-link fence, inexplicable and rusting, encompasses the compound. The strands of barbed-wire that run along the top edge of the fence are taut and oddly slanted inward, like those of a prison might be—to keep the inmates in, not intruders out. The few cars scattered about are mostly small and aging; most have dented bodies or broken taillights or some missing part. The edges of an opaque plastic garbage bag are taped to the frame of one of them where the rear window was; the plastic is loose, collecting water from the rain, sagging under the weight. Another sits, tire-less, on concrete blocks between the buildings.

In the middle building, on the second floor, a young child stands barefoot by a window peering out into the grayness. The room is cold from the dampness, and a wide brown stain running down from the ceiling on one wall is slowly spreading and darkens as the rain continues. There is not a bulb in the lamp in the corner, so the ambient light from the window offers the only illumination to the dim, shadowy room.

The child, a boy not much more than a toddler, plops down beside the window. The floor is covered by light-brown carpet, dirty and stained. In several places, the synthetic material has been melted into small dark circles by the fallen ashes from cigarettes. The child spies something outside, across the way from his window and seems mesmerized by it.

"Jadie, where are you? What are you doing, baby?" The voice, hoarse and reedy, comes from down the short hallway, from the bedroom. The thin voice is familiar to the child, but he doesn't respond. He just sits on the filthy floor, in the damp cold, staring out the window.

"Jadie, sweetheart, come here," she calls out again. The child doesn't move. Maybe he doesn't hear her. "Jadie."

Finally, with great effort, the woman pushes herself up and rests on an elbow against the bed. She coughs, ragged and deep, and reaches for the switch of the small lamp beside the bed. With a click, the low-watt bulb casts inadequate, yellow light about the room. Finally, with great effort, she sits up on the edge of the bed. She is not an old woman and her finely etched features suggest that at one time she may have been pretty, or near it. But now her brown hair is dull and pulled back, accentuating the gaunt face, the dark sunken eyes, and the paleness of her almost translucent skin. She coughs again and reaches for the pack of cigarettes on the bedside table, pushing aside the various pill bottles. Some spill out onto the floor. With a shallow sigh of disappointment, she crushes the empty pack in her thin, shaking hand and drops it back onto the table.

She rises slowly, steadying herself with a hand against the wall of the small room. From the foot of the bed she gropes for a thin, pink robe and wraps it around her and makes her way down the hallway to where the child is.

"There you are, my sweet boy. What are you doing? Do you see something out the window?" The little boy looks up at her as she balances herself, and with painful effort the woman settles on the sofa. "Come here, Jadie. Let momma hold you." The child stands up and points to something outside.

"Doggie," he says.

"Oh, you see the dog. Come here and tell momma about it. What you see. Is it a good dog?"

The child walks slowly over to his mother. Without her assistance, he climbs into her lap. She hugs him tightly, as tightly as she is able. He then looks up at her and touches her face lightly with small dirty fingers.

"I love you, Jadie. I love you so much," she says.

The child doesn't respond, but slides from her lap back onto the floor. From a small stack of frayed and worn Little Golden Books on the floor near the window, he grasps one of them and holds it up for his mother to see. She nods. He goes to her and she takes the thin book from him and looks at it and smiles. The boy crawls back up onto the sofa and settles onto her lap. She begins to read to him. He listens, but looks beyond her, to the window. It is raining harder now and the huge drops beat a steady rhythm against the glass.

After a short while, she begins to cough again. She holds the child tight, nearly expending the little strength she has. She finishes the story and places the book beside her on the sofa. The boy slides off her lap again onto the floor and brings her another book. He stands and looks up at her, holding the thin book up for her to see.

"Oh, Jadie, I can't right now. I'll go lie down for a little while and then I'll read you another story. In a while, I promise. And then we'll have some supper."

It is a struggle for her to rise from the sofa and make her way back to the bedroom. She wants a cigarette very badly. What difference does it make now, she thinks. Then she is gone. The boy returns to the window, and to the rain, and to the sad brown dog across the way.

CHAPTER 1

The car slowed, but not enough to keep it from skidding to a stop in the gravel beside the two rusting gasoline pumps which were probably inoperable, as they had pumped no fuel in a long time. The driver, a heavy-set man in uniform, exited the cruiser and made his way to the screen-doored entrance of the small, cinder block building. It stood, low and alone, at the corner of the recently asphalted county highway and a dirt road.

"Howdy," said the thin, toothless woman sitting on a stool behind the counter. Her new dentures did not fit properly and cut into her gums. She had removed them and placed them in a glass of turbid water on the narrow shelf behind her.

"How to do," returned the policeman, letting the screen door slam shut behind him.

"Hot, ain't it?"

"Hot as blazes. Dry, too. We could use some rain." He removed his visored cap and wiped his forehead with the back of his hand.

"Yeah, we could. What can I help you with?" She did not move from the stool.

"Sign says you got the best hot dogs in town. That so?"

"They's good as you can get 'round here."

"And just what *town* might your sign be referring to? You way up in the hills here."

"Just a figure of speech, I reckon. Town's Russellville. You'd of come through it a ways back."

"Yeah, guess I did at that. Not much of a town though."

"No, not much of one. You want a hotdog?"

"I reckon I *will* have one if they as good as you say they are."

She slid down off the stool and moved over to the small two-burner stove behind the counter.

"Whatcha want on it?"

"Got chili?"

"Course I got chili!"

"Okay, give me one with chili and onions and yellow mustard."

"One all the way, then?"

"Yep, all the way."

"You can have a seat at one of them tables there behind you. I'll bring it out to you. Drink box is over in the corner," she said, throwing a glance to an old, red metal cooler back of the store.

"Thanks. Got Tom's Orange?"

"I do, but my hotdogs is best with Pepsi. Least that's what folks around here tell me."

"I'll have a Tom's Orange." He opened the top of the drink box. It was the old-fashioned kind with the bottled drinks submerged in icy water. Much of the ice had melted, but the water was still cold. He reached in and pulled out a bottle of Tom's Orange, opening it with the bottle opener attached to the side of the box. He then rubbed the wet hand down the side of his trousers and sat down on one of the benches attached to either side of the table. They were, fact, heavy picnic tables with red and white checkered oilcloths covering them.

"You want some chips with this?" she called over to him, but did not look up from her work preparing the hotdog.

"Got fries?"

"No, I don't cook fries. Too messy."

"Then I reckon I'll have chips," he said.

"They in a rack there behind you there. Help yourself."

He turned sideways on the bench and reached over and pulled of a small bag of potato chips clipped to a metal display stand. She came around from the counter and placed the hotdog, loosely wrapped in wax paper, on the table before him.

"Be anything else, Sheriff?"

"I'm not a sheriff," he said as he chomped the hotdog.

"Car says sheriff. Wofford County." She was standing looking out the screen door.

"Actin' sheriff," he said as he chewed. He took a gulp of the orange soda.

"Whatcha doing over here in McBee County. I know it ain't none of my business, just wonderin'."

"Lookin' around."

"You official *lookin'* or just killin' time?"

"I ain't got jurisdiction in McBee County." He swallowed the last bite.

"Unofficial, then."

"Yeah, unofficial." He pulled a paper napkin from the metal dispenser on the table and wiped his mouth. "I'll take another one of them dogs if you don't mind."

"Told you they was good," she said and gave a toothless grin. "Sure thing, another one all the way coming up."

He rose from the table and walked over and leaned on the counter, watching her fix his order.

"Don't seem like you get many folks in here," he said.

"Not in the middle of the afternoon. Got a pretty big lunch crowd, though. House painters and the fence boys stop by in the mornin's for beer, loggers in the evenin's."

"Sounds like mostly local folks," he said.

"Pretty much," she said as she handed him the hotdog across the counter. "There you go, Sheriff."

"Thanks."

He returned to the bench at the table. He brushed away a black housefly and drained the last of the soda from the bottle. Finishing the hotdog quickly, he balled the wax paper into a tight wad and tossed it into the waste basket beside the table. She was watching him.

"Just leave the bottle. I'll pick it up when I wipe down the table."

"All right," he said, suppressing a soft burp with a fist. "Those *were* right good hotdogs." He approached the counter. "How much I owe you?"

"Let's see, now. Hotdog's a dollar fifty and you had a drank. Did you have just one bag of chips?"

"Yeah, one."

"That'll be four-fifty, I reckon."

He placed a five-dollar bill on the counter. She rang up the charge and slid two quarters change back across the counter.

"Let me ask you something," he said, his fingers toying with the coins.

"What?" She leaned forward, both hands on the cash register.

"Been anybody come by your store lately that maybe you didn't know? A stranger?"

She hesitated, still looking at him. "This 'bout that girl they found up on Sadler's Creek, ain't it?"

"Might be."

"The police done been up here and asked me a whole bunch of questions. I don't know anything. That's what I told them and that's what I'm tellin' you."

"Nobody been in but your regulars, then?"

"That's right. Just folks I know." She rolled her lips between her gums. "That young'un was the only one that weren't."

"A young'un, you say?"

"Ah, just a boy come in late that mornin', I think it was. Didn't say much. Kinda snooty. I don't know, maybe he was just bashful. Bought a pack of Nabs and left."

"Was he on foot?"

"He was. Took off up the dirt road there. Goin' fishing, I reckon."

"That right?"

"Said he was. He was totin' a fishing pole. Not a pole. You know, uh, a rod and reel."

"Sadler's Creek up that dirt road?" The Deputy motioned toward the window that overlooked the road.

"Yep, that's where he was headed, I reckon."

"Did you tell the police about the Boy?"

"Well, no I didn't. To tell you the truth I plumb forgot about it. Anyway, I didn't like 'em much. Kinda pushy and rude. Big city boys, you know what I mean?"

"Yeah, I know what you mean. But you might better tell them about it if they come back around."

"I don't 'spec they will. This about that girl got killed, ain't it? I mean that's why you over here in McBee County."

He gave a slight shrug, and without answering her question, turned and strode toward the door. He then stopped and walked over to the table where he had eaten the hotdogs and placed the two quarters on the table. They looked at each other, he and the woman, but neither spoke. He pushed open the screen door, got into the patrol car, and drove away. Through the smudged and dingy side window, she watched him turn onto the dirt road toward Sadler's Creek.

CHAPTER 2

From the tar and gravel road you could see the faded blue house trailer below. A narrow dirt path ran down from the road across a wide, slanted field of broom sedge, tangled briars, and scrubby jack pine. The path led to the trailer, not straight but meandering, as the earth here was eroded and gashed with deep, red-clay gullies. When it rained, the red soil washed down the gullies into the river, the mud turning it a seething, dingy, reddish brown. In dry weather, the river flowed slower and the murky water took on the lighter color of heavily-creamed coffee.

The isolated trailer was on a low bluff above the river and rested on concrete blocks just beyond a shallow, but ever-widening gully. Oddly, its front door faced the gully and the field and the road above, not the river. More concrete blocks, chipped and gray, served as steps to the front door. An old South Bend rod, the fiberglass cracked and peeling, with an open-faced reel leaned against the aluminum siding beside the steps.

The Boy shuffled from his room rubbing the sleep from his eyes, and plopped down on the over-sized, brown Naugahyde sofa. The flimsy, aluminum-framed living room window had been raised and a wobbly overhead fan rotated slowly and rattled a monotonous rhythm.

"Well, did you git your nap out?" asked the heavy-set woman without looking up from the TV show she was watching. The Boy did not respond. "Ain't nothing left to eat. I already cleaned up the kitchen."

"I don't want nothing," he said.

"They's a can of Campbell's soup you can warm over for your lunch, I reckon."

"I ain't hungry."

"Well, you just might be in a hour or two." She looked over at him. "Anyway, I need you to go out and weed my tomatoes. Do it before it gets hot."

"It's already hot. Besides, I'm going fishing," the Boy replied without shifting from his slumped position on the sofa.

"You can go fishing if you want to. I don't care what you do, just weed my tomatoes first."

"I ain't weedin' no tomatoes today," he said, without emotion.

"Damn, boy, you 'bout sorry as your daddy was. Don't want nothing to do with no work, that's for sure. I reckon a couple of years on the chain gang might cure that lazy streak in him though," she said flatly, shifting her gaze back to the TV.

"Why you always got to bring him up? I ain't him."

"You ain't him yet, but you well on your way. I'll never know what your mama saw in that man. I declare, I don't."

"She must've seen something. She married him."

"That she did, and regretted every day afterward I 'spect. Tried to talk her out of it, but she wouldn't listen to nothing I had to say. He was a smooth talker, that one. But she was a good girl. Deserved better."

"I don't want to talk about her neither," said the Boy. He wasn't sure he could remember his mother. He had a vague, dream-like memory of sitting on a woman's lap and her maybe reading to him or something. And rain. He remembered rain. It may have been his mother, but it was a long time ago. He could not have been much more than a baby. He tried hard to remember, but couldn't. He couldn't make out her face, which was the thing that troubled him most. But maybe that was a good thing—he didn't know. He always imagined her beautiful. Maybe it *was* a dream.

"She was my little sister. Reckon I'll talk about her if I want to. Ain't no young'un goin' to tell me what I can or can't talk about."

"It's always the same old thing with you. 'Your daddy was sorry as hell but your mama was like an angel on earth'," he said, mimicking his aunt's voice. "I'm tired of hearin' it."

"I don't care what you tired of. I reckon you tired of me, too."

The Boy grew silent, watching with bored disinterest the smiling, jabbering people on the TV screen. The aunt lit a cigarette, coughed hoarsely, and exhaled a plume of bluish white smoke into the hot, stuffy living room. With great effort, she reached down and picked up something off the stained, frayed carpet. She examined it closely in her fingers.

"Damn it all, looks like we got rats again," she said, brushing her hands together several time. "Reckon I better go and wash my hands." With effort, she pulled herself up out of the stuffed chair and padded off to the bathroom down the narrow hallway.

The Boy went back into his room and pulled on jeans and a threadbare tee shirt. He tied his sneakers and took a dollar from the small dresser drawer beside his unmade bed. When he returned to the living room his aunt had resumed her position in front of the TV. He looked out the back window at the river.

"Well, if you bound to go fishing you can dig some worms around the rose bushes. I sure wish you'd weed them tomatoes though."

"I know where the worms are. Don't need you tellin' me something I already know. Besides, I ain't fishing with worms today."

"Okay, Mister Know-it-all, how you goin' to fish without no worms?"

"I'm goin' use that can corn that's in the kitchen cabinet. The niblet corn."

"Ain't no catfish goin' to bite corn, niblet or otherwise."

"I'm tired of fishing that muddy old river, catchin' nothing but catfish," he said.

"Seems you getting tired of just about everything around here."

"I'm tired of catfish." And I'm tired of you too, he thought.

"Well, there's a few bream in there, too. You can catch bream sometimes. I bet they'd bite at corn." She lit another cigarette and pointed the remote toward the TV, with a click.

"I'm goin' fishing for trout," he said.

"Trout? You crazy, boy. Ain't no trout fish in that river."

"You reckon I don't know that? I'm goin' to hike up to Sadler's Creek. It's good, clean water, maybe cold enough for trout. Trout need that kind of water." He didn't know what kind of water trout needed, but it sounded right.

"Why you want to go and do something that like for? Catfish ain't good enough for you now, is that it? Got to go trout fishing."

"I'm just tired of fishing in the river, that's all. Nothing wrong with that."

"Where's this here Sadler's Creek you talkin' about?"

"Up in the hills, past Russellville. It's a mountain creek," he said.

"Russellville? That's a long way to walk just to go fishing."

"I know some short cuts. I don't mind the walkin'."

"Something you want to do, you'll up and do it right off. I ask you to help me around here, it's like pullin' teeth." She drew on the cigarette deeply and then exhaled. "How'd you know about that creek anyhow?"

"I just know, that's all."

He went into the narrow galley kitchen and took a small can of Green Giant niblet corn from the cupboard. He walked back through the living room to the front door. The fat woman turned and looked up at him from where she sat.

"I can't go furnishin' you with a can of corn every time you want to go *trout* fishing," she said. "My check only goes so far. Especially now I got two mouths to feed."

"You get money for me, too."

"Maybe I do, but it still ain't enough."

He did not respond. He shoved the can of corn into his pocket, stepped out of the trailer into the sunlight, grabbed the rod and reel, and was gone.

There was a rough path he knew that ran across the field and into the woods. It met the county road just north of Russellville, on the creek side. The air was hot and still, and the dry twigs and leaves crunched beneath his sneakers as he walked. It was the only sound in the dark, languid air of the forest.

When he first left the trailer that morning he was thinking of his aunt. He thought how fat and ugly she was. Always just lounging around in dirty flannel pajamas or sweat pants, smoking and watching TV. She did not want him there; he knew that well enough. And he did not want to have to stay with her, but it was, in most ways at least, better than it had been at the foster home. And the beatings. He had this vague, inexplicable feeling that maybe he somehow had deserved it; he didn't know. Then he remembered the day his caseworker had taken him there—delivered him to the door like he was a mail-order package. First, they had cleaned him up really good, even got a haircut, and put new shoes on his feet—new to him, anyway.

He is looking down at the floorboard, at the new shoes, as they pull up to the curb and he does not look up when the car stops. The house is a dull, dark place with a sad, twisted water oak growing in the dirt yard. Thin, wiry, vines snake their way up the peeling clapboard siding of the house, reaching almost to the sagging gutters along the edge of the roof. Two people, a man and a woman, sit in unpainted rockers in the shadows on the porch.

"Now don't this look like a real nice place? And there's your new foster mama and daddy on the porch just waiting for you. I think you'll like it here," the caseworker says with a forced cheerfulness.

I don't like her, he thinks, she just wants to be rid of me. She is dark-skinned and emaciated, and has hardly spoken to him up until now. When she does say something her voice is dry and impatient, telling him to do this or that, or not do this or that. She is always talking to someone on the phone about his file while he sits in her office or outside in the waiting room. He remembers the smell of cheap disinfectant and cigarettes. He can still hear her thin, reedy voice. His file. He knows that he has become nothing more than a name on a thick, greasy manila folder. There is a number beside his name.

She holds his hand tightly as they walk through the hard, dusty yard to the porch steps. As though he might try to escape. He cannot remember anyone ever holding his hand before and he does not like the clammy dampness of her bony fingers wrapped around his.

"Good afternoon," says the caseworker.

The woman on the porch rises from the rocker to greet them. The man does not get up, but the Boy sees him and knows he is eyeing him.

"Well, my, my, this must be Jadie," the woman says. "He's a nice looking young feller. Y'all come on in and we'll get acquainted."

"Yes, ma'am, this here is Jadie all right and he's really glad to be coming to stay with y'all. He's a good boy, all things considered," the caseworker says, her practiced smile tight and fake. "Jadie, this here is Mrs. Galloway, your new foster mama."

He winces slightly when Mrs. Galloway touches his shoulder as he steps up onto the porch; the caseworker is close behind. Then the woman, his new foster mama, speaks to the man in the rocker.

"Bud, hon, come on over here and meet Jadie, our new boy." The man turns his head away and spits a stream of brown tobacco juice over the bannister into the yard. He *doesn't move from the chair. "Oh, don't mind him. He's just quare."*

As it turned out, the Galloway's, at least Mrs. Galloway, were "professional" foster parents. That is, they took in children for the money the state social services paid them each month. Jadie soon learned that there were two more children in the house—girls both younger than him. Mr. Galloway stayed drunk most of the time, and mean all of the time. He never went off someplace to drink, but rather retreated to a dilapidated shed out back of the house. After supper he usually retired to the shed where he took down a bottle from a high shelf and began to drink from it.

Sometimes at first, before dark, Jadie sneaks out to the shed. Through the cracks of the planked wall, he watches Mr. Galloway guzzle the liquor as he slumps mumbling in a beat-up old aluminum lawn chair with much of the strapping torn and hanging down loose. The Boy never tells anyone about his doing this—watching the old man get drunk—and he doesn't really consider it to be great fun. Just odd and not much interesting; that's all. Something to do.

Often the man passes out, sprawled in the lawn chair, and sleeps there all night. Come morning he stumbles in the back door and sits down heavily at the kitchen table. His wife brings his breakfast to him. She pours coffee into a mug beside his plate, but the Boy never sees him touch it. At first, with the two girls sitting at the table he does not acknowledge them. But shortly after the Boy arrives he begins to stare at him as he wolfs down the greasy eggs his wife places in front of him. His eyes are pools of dark contempt and a nameless hatred seems to swirl around in them. Sometimes he curls his lips in a snarl and curses in a barely audible voice. The Boy listens and hears him and smells the vile breath, but he doesn't look at the man. No one talks. Nothing ever happens in the mornings.

Sometimes while in his shed Galloway is roused from his alcoholic coma by a late car passing on the street, a distant siren, or some other inconsequential noise. If he fully wakes he leaves the shed and comes into the house. The house is still and quiet. Mrs. Galloway and the children are asleep except for the Boy. He hears the screen door slam shut and then he knows. He hears the drunkard's heavy, falling footsteps as he makes his way across the kitchen, pushing chairs aside clumsily and cursing as he stumbles in the darkness. Lying on the narrow fold-out cot in the small side room—not much more than a closet—the Boy listens as the man approaches from down the hallway. Most of the time, at first at least, Galloway staggers on past Jadie's room to the end of the hallway. This is where Mrs. Galloway sleeps. He wonders if she, too, is awake as her drunk husband approaches.

But occasionally, and it becomes more frequent, he hears the footsteps stop and he knows the man is just outside his door. He freezes and pulls the dank quilt up to his chin, hoping Galloway will walk on by. Sometimes he just shuffles on down the hall and the Boy strains to listen as the footsteps stop again. Galloway must be at the door of the little girls' room. They seem to be more terrified of him with each passing day. At breakfast they hold their heads down and stare at their plates. They do not look at him. They do not touch their food.

Then comes the night he doesn't move away from the Boy's door. He remembers the first time. Galloway opens the door, pushing hard against it, causing it to slam it against the wall. He doesn't switch on the light, but rather stands swaying over the child, cursing and slobbering, his breathing heavy and foul. He suddenly reaches down and yanks the Boy from the bed and begins to shake him violently, his cursing growing louder and louder. Then the slapping begins. Back and forth across the young face, the huge open hand smacking sharply as bone and flesh meet.

By this time, Mrs. Galloway is in the doorway screaming and begging her husband to stop the beating. The young girls huddle together outside on the floor in the hallway, sobbing. Finally, it is over. Galloway rudely shoves the Boy back onto the cot. He then brushes Mrs. Galloway aside and stumbles down the hallway to his own room, slamming the bedroom door behind him.

Mrs. Galloway rushes over, sobbing, and kneels beside the cot.

"Oh, honey, I'm so sorry. Are you all right?"

No answer comes, just the sound of the Boy's shallow, rapid breathing.

"I'm sorry he hurt you. He didn't mean it. He just gets this way sometimes when he's a- drinking. He won't do it again, I promise. He just gets too drunk, that's all. I'll talk to him in the morning. When he's feeling better. All right?"

She sobs as she strokes the Boy's forehead. He does not respond, but lies there in the darkness as the numbness fades away, to be replaced by pain. Finally, thinking he had drifted off to sleep, she gets up and pads off toward the bedroom. He hears the loud, obnoxious snoring of Galloway. Through it all, the Boy never makes a sound.

It will be two years and more beatings before Galloway shoots his wife in the temple with a pistol as she sleeps beside him. He then shoots himself. The thin, black social worker comes in the night, blurry-eyed and grumpy, along with a policeman, and takes him away. He doesn't know what becomes of the little girls. He just knows that he will never see them again.

CHAPTER 3

At least his aunt didn't beat him. Hell, she's too lazy to, he thought. And she didn't make him go to school when he didn't want to go either. That didn't seem right to him though he didn't mind it much. The people in the foster home had made him go to school every day, but he figured they had to since the social worker would drop by the house at odd times and ask them how he was doing. He thought he saw her at the school once, but he wasn't sure it was her. She had never come to the trailer by the river.

She was fat and ugly, his aunt, and he hated her. Her white, soft flesh protruding over the waistband of the gray sweat pants she wore disgusted him. He had dreams once about her in which she died horribly and wasn't there anymore. Then a quick thought, maybe *he* would kill her. Could he do it? He sighed and shook off the thought like a bad dream. Then he forgot about her.

Finally, at the edge of the woods, he came to a shallow ditch and jumped across it onto the narrow shoulder of the county road. He immediately spotted the store in the distance on the other side, up to his left and started for it, the can of niblet corn joggling in his jeans pocket. His tee shirt was damp with perspiration, but his throat was dry and he was very thirsty. He tried to spit but couldn't; cotton-mouth, he thought.

He crossed over and walked along the edge of the road to where a narrow dirt road led up into the woods beside the store. As he strode onto the dusty gravel yard of the store, he spotted a faucet near the rear corner of the building. He walked over and knelt down beside it. When he twisted the weathered green-brass spigot, there was a low hiss of air and then a sputtering stream of brown rust-colored water. He let it run for a moment until the water cleared and flowed freely. He put his mouth to the faucet, and gulped down the tepid liquid.

When he entered the store the woman was perched on a high stool behind the counter. He closed the screen door softly behind him. They looked at each other.

"Hello, sonny," she said.

"Hey," he said, almost inaudibly.

"Can I help you?"

"No, I'm just goin' to get me some crackers or something."

"Crackers and candy are back there in that rack beside the drink box."

She returned to reading the magazine spread open on the counter in front of her. The Boy walked back toward the rear of the store.

"How much are these cheese crackers," he asked, not looking back at her.

"Them peanut butter cheese crackers?"

"Yes."

"Them's Nabs and they fifty-cent a pack."

He took the pack of crackers up to the counter, the rod and reel held in one hand at his side. With the other he pulled the wrinkled dollar bill from his pocket and placed it on the counter beside the newspaper. She slid down off the stool and rang up the sale.

"There you go, fifty-cent change. I won't charge you no tax this time," she grinned, but the Boy did not reply. He just scooped up the two quarters and dropped them into his pocket. They clinked against the can of niblet corn.

"Looks like you might be goin' fishing. Headed up to the creek?"

"Yeah, I guess so."

"Well, if it's Sadler's Creek where you headed it's up that dirt road there".

"I know where it is," he said in a flat, young voice.

"Well, I reckon you do at that. Just tryin' to be helpful, that's all."

Without speaking, he turned and left the store. As he walked up the dirt road, he tore open the cellophane wrapper that held the crackers and began to munch on one.

He hadn't fished for trout before nor had he ever seen one, not in person anyway. One time when he was sitting outside the social worker's office there were some magazines, all out of date and tattered, on the table. Out of boredom, he picked one up. On the cover was the rendering of a large colorful fish leaping out of a crystal-clear stream. There was a hook in the corner of its mouth attached to a taut line which ran to a deeply bowed rod held by a man with a stupid grin on his tanned face. He had caught plenty of catfish and carp. He remembered the one time, before he went to jail, his father came to see him at the foster home. It was on a Sunday. Standing at the front door on the porch, he saw him hand Mrs. Galloway some money—dollar bills. Then they, he and his father, got into an old pickup truck and drove to a small pond where you paid to fish from the bank. With a tight wad of cotton and dough for bait strung from a bamboo pole, the heavy bait quickly sank and you could catch the bottom-feeders lurking there in the muddy water.

In a few minutes he felt a tug on the line. Nothing quick or exciting, but a tug—a bite. He jerked the cane pole up and his daddy grabbed the line.

"I believe you got one, boy. I purely and surely do. I'll just help you bring him in here," his daddy said, as he pulled the line in with his hand.

And there was a fish, a big cat fish, hanging at the end of the line, the hook set deep in its gullet. But he remembered thinking, I didn't do nothing. Just baited my hook and dropped it over the bank, into the water. And waited. I didn't do nothing.

"That's a good 'un, son," his father had said. "A real good'un."

They had fished for a while longer and caught some more fish, but nothing like the first one. His daddy kept pulling cans of beer from the cooler he had brought, downing them one after the other until finally he seemed to lose interest in the fishing. It had been a good day, at least for him. Late in the day he asked his father if he could come live with him, maybe for a little while.

"I don't know about that, son," his daddy replied. "We'll see."

But nothing ever came of it. Late in the day they gathered up their stuff, mostly empty beer cans, and left the pay-for-fishing pond and drove back to the foster home. His father pulled the truck up in the yard and they just sat there. Finally, his daddy turned and said, "Well, I got to go now. I guess we had a pretty good time today. Caught some fish. You best go on in. It's about supper time."

"All right," the Boy replied. "Can we do this again soon? Come take me fishing, I mean."

"Sure I will."

He then got out of the truck and walked to the house. He stopped on the steps to the porch and turned to wave to his father. But his daddy had already backed the truck out of the yard and pulled onto the street; he didn't look back. That was the last time he saw him.

Fishing with his daddy had been fun in a way and they had caught a few catfish. But he had never seen anything like the fish on the magazine cover. It looked so alive and beautiful. So he read the article as best he could. The fish was a rainbow trout and these fish were plentiful in many of the mountain streams. Streams somewhere, it didn't say. The water had to be clear, swift, and cold. He read about using artificial flys as bait, but dismissed that concept out of hand as being too fancy and difficult for him. Anyway, where would he even get them. The piece went on to describe people who fished for these trout using unethical, or at least unsportsmanlike, methods. They fished with live bait or canned corn. They used spinning rigs, not fly rods. Most even kept all the fish they caught if they could get away with it. That is, if they could evade the game warden.

He did not understand everything in the article, but he knew that someday he wanted to catch a trout. He had forgotten about this until much later when his aunt had brought home the can of niblet corn along with other groceries. Seeing the can of corn reminded him of what he had seen in the magazine. He didn't have or need artificial flies. He knew how to catch fish so he figured he would know how to catch trout.

He tied the ends of the shoelaces together and draped the sneakers around his neck so that they hung down loosely against his chest. The man on the magazine cover had been standing in the water so he figured that must be the best way to catch trout. He rolled the cuffs of his jeans up to his knees and waded into the swift, broad stream—Sadler's Creek. The mountain water, cold and alien, swirled against his skin.

At first, he struggled to maintain his balance as his bare feet slipped on the smooth, slick rocks covering the stream bed. But with the strength and reflexes of youth, he quickly gained control of his movements and was steady enough to slide a piece of the niblet corn onto the barb of the hook. He expertly cast the line and retrieved it slowly, turning the reel handle lightly with his fingers. He repeated this several times without results. He then decided to cast downstream and let the hook sink to the bottom and just lie there, the way that he caught catfish.

The air was cooler up here and he felt a vague pleasantness with the water swirling around his thin legs. Except for an occasional bird chirping and the gentle resonance of the stream itself, the world was silent. It seemed a million miles from the foster homes and his hideous aunt.

He eventually found a rhythm to casting the line, waiting a few moments then slowly retrieving it. By doing this he made his way slowly downstream. The stream became swifter, with larger moss-covered rocks protruding from its turbulent surface. Now well away from the low bank where he had first entered the water, the bank now rose eight or ten feet high on either side—a small canyon cut into the earth by centuries of the natural flow of the creek. Hickory trees, tall and stately, bordered the banks and cedars and rhododendron grew lush in the dark, damp soil among them. He could smell the cedars.

He had just cast the line when the stillness was broken by a voice, almost a growl, that came from behind him. High up.

"What ye doin' down there, boy?"

Somewhat startled, he turned to see three people, two men and a woman, standing on the bank's edge above him. The larger man, the one who had called out, wore a dingy brown felt hat pushed back on his forehead. The other man was thin, almost emaciated, and hatless. Standing between them was a woman. She was thin and young, not much more than a girl. She wore shorts—cutoff jeans—with ragged unhemmed edges. Her hair was long, dull and lank, and seemed almost colorless. Unlike the two men, she was shoeless and on her sleeveless, black tee shirt were the words, 'Shit Happens', in yellow.

Behind them the high sun shot shafts of light through the trees and the Boy squinted to try and make out the faces. The small, thin man kept trying to put his arm around the girl's waist, but she giggled and squirmed free, pushing him away. The Boy turned back to his fishing.

"You deft or something, boy? I asked ye a question," the Big man yelled down again. He could hear the girl giggling.

"Just fishing. I reckon you can see that much."

"Oh, I believe we got us a smart aleck here." The Small man and the girl snickered. "Catch anything, boy?"

"Not yet," he replied, still facing downstream, away from the trio on the bank.

The Big man pulled a pint bottle from his back pocket and drank from it. He passed it to the girl and the Small man. Each took a drink.

"Yer want a drink of likker, boy?" This from the thin man.

"No sir, I don't drink," the Boy said.

"He don't drink," said the girl mockingly, giggling. "I guess all you do is fish, then." Guffaws from the two men.

"We headed up to that meader a little piece other side the creek. We goin' to have us a little party," the girl called out, again pushing the Small man back away from her. "Why don't you come with us and have some fun. I ain't sure these two ole boys here can handle what all I got for 'em, if you know what I mean."

The Boy retrieved the line and cast it again. He did not reply nor look back up at them. The Big man took another drink from the bottle.

"Looky here, boy." The young Boy ignored him.

"I said, looky here! Or you want a ass-whuppin"? he shouted, louder.

The Boy turned toward them. He wasn't afraid of the Big man or the other one either. They're drunk, he thought. I'd be long gone before they could get down the bank after me. They likely couldn't run anyway.

"Hey, boy, you ever had any?" he asked.

"I told you I don't drink whiskey," he said.

"Hell, boy, I ain't talkin' about whiskey," the Big man laughed, the other man grinned and swayed unsteadily. The girl twirled strands of her limp hair with her fingers and pursed her lips looking down at him. She was no longer giggling. The Boy stared back at her.

Finally, she said, "Come, boys, he ain't nothing but a kid. Let's go on up yonder to the meader."

"Yeah, let's go have some fun," said the Small man. "Gimme another sup of that likker."

The Big man passed him the bottle and placed his arm around the girl's shoulder. She did not attempt to remove it.

"That kid live around here somewhere?" he asked the girl.

"How the hell would I know. I ain't never seen him before," she slurred and pulled on his arm. "Let's git goin' and have some fun. Gimme another slug of that whiskey, too."

"Wait jis' a minute," said the Big man, pushing her away. He called down to the Boy, "Where you live at, boy?"

The Boy hesitated, looking downstream. He wanted to be left alone. Just catch a trout or two and walk back home. He did not like these people. The two men didn't bother much him, but the girl scared him a little. He wasn't sure why. He felt an uneasiness when he looked up at her on the bank, just standing there, looking down at him. Then he thought, just answer him and maybe they'll move on.

"I live over yonder by the river," the Boy said.

"What river?"

"Just the river, that's all," the Boy said and began to move away, downstream from the trio.

"Leave him be. He ain't nothing but a scrawny-ass kid. You a man, ain't you?" the girl swayed and giggled. The Small man kept looking at her, biting his lower lip.

"Come on," he said, "I'm ready to go."

The three of them turned and walked back upstream along the bank, and soon disappeared into the woods.

For a few moments the Boy could hear the girl's throaty giggling and the Small man's high pitched voice, mostly curses. He remembered what she had said to him. It made him feel funny, but not unpleasant. There was something about it. Something he didn't understand it. As the voices drifted away he reeled in the line and moved further downstream.

By late afternoon he was tired and thirsty. Wading in the creek all day, the back of his neck ached with sunburn. Should have tied a rag around my neck, he thought, when I felt it burning me. He reeled in the line and splashed from the creek and sat on the bank. He had caught no trout. Maybe there were no trout in Sadler's Creek. Maybe catching trout was harder than he thought it would be. Looked easy for the man on the magazine cover. But he wouldn't give up. He'd come back to the creek soon. Maybe tomorrow.

He pushed himself up off the damp ground, picked up the rod and reel, and walked upstream along the edge. He had meandered down the creek, fishing, much farther than he had realized. He'd need to find the dirt road soon if he was going to make it home before dark. He had not thought any more about the two men and the woman until now. He did not want to run into them again. For a moment he pictured the girl standing barefoot up on the bank looking down at him, slowly twisting strands of hair with her fingers. He picked up his pace and then decided to cut through the woods. He knew about where the road should be.

Quicker than he thought, he reached the end of the dirt road where it intersected with the paved county road. The store was off to his right and there were several pickup trucks parked in front. He remembered the spigot and strode over to drink from it. He wished he had money for a cold Pepsi. He then crossed the road and walked down it until he found the path that led into the woods, and home.

As he approached the trailer in the twilight he could see the flickering of the TV through the dingy front window. The light cast vague, irregular shadows on the wall inside. His aunt was in her recliner. He wondered if she had moved from the TV all day. Probably not. She would give him hell for not having caught any fish. He leaned the rod and reel against the trailer beside the steps and went inside.

"There you are," she said, barely glancing away from the TV screen. "I was gettin' worried about you."

"You don't look worried."

"Well, I was. Some, anyway. Where you been?"

"You know where I been," he said.

"Oh, yeah, that's right. You been fishing. Doing that damned fancy trout fishing."

The Boy did not respond and stood looking at the inane game show blaring on the television across the room. Finally, his aunt turned him and said, "Well?"

"Well what?"

"Where's all them fish you was goin' to catch?" she asked.

"I didn't have no luck," he said, his voice thin and flat.

"I didn't figure you would. You ain't got no business wanderin' off up in them hills."

"I wasn't wanderin'. I knew where I was goin'."

"Say, you got some l'il ole girl you meeting up there in the woods, have you?" she chuckled lewdly.

The young woman with the lank, mouse-colored hair flashed across his mind. He could see her clearly, but strangely the two men were not there in his mind's eye.

"Naw, I ain't got no girl. I just went fishing. Is there anything to eat for supper?"

"I ain't felt real good today. Sure didn't feel like cookin'. There's a TV dinner in the freezer. You can eat it if you're hungry."

"All right," he said. He got up and walked into the kitchen.

From the road you could not see the flames of the small campfire deep in the woods, its flames flickering and dancing low to the ground. In late August in the South, nights are often hot and breezeless, the air heavy and sultry from the merciless sun of the day. There was nothing for a fire to do but provide light in the thick darkness of the forest. Two men were at it, one squatted on the ground, his back to a straight, but dead pine tree. The other hovered nearer the fire, rocking back and forth on his haunches inexplicably warming his hands above the flames. These were not good men. The yellow light flickered across their faces like an old movie newsreel, gaunt faces showing the dark stubble of several day's growth. The thick, dead air of the night had silenced the usual cricket chirping, so the only constant sounds were those of the low, crackling fire and the heavy, slow breathing of the two men. Occasionally, the muted sound of a passing car or the whine of big truck tires was heard faintly from the distant county road.

The Small man, the one over the fire, seemed nervous. He constantly looked around the clearing into the darkness with quick jerky movements of his head.

"What you so jumpy about?" asked the one leaning against the pine, watching him.

"I ain't jumpy. Jis' being watchful, that's all."

"What ye watchin' out for?"

"I don't know. You know, nothin'. What the hell? I sure could use a drink, if they's any left."

"Ain't none, it's gone. You gettin' the shakes already?"

"Some, I reckon," said the Small man.

They both fell silent, staring into the fire. A rare breeze, slight and warm, teased the trees tops high above. The Small man glanced up into the darkness.

"Damn cool for August, ain't it?"

"It's hotter than hell. You just got the chills along with them shakes. That's all it is. Fire'll keep ye from freezin' to death," the Big man said with a smirk.

"Ground feelin' cold. Be hard to sleep on tonight."

"Ye can pile up some of them pine needles by the fire. You'll sleep all right."

"I'm hungry."

"Yeah, me too." The Big man slid down from his squatting to sit on the ground, his back still against the pine. For a while neither spoke.

"Damn quiet out here, ain't it," said the Small man, gazing into the flames.

"Good thing it is. We can hear somebody a comin'."

"You don't reckon nobody would be out here this time of night, do you? I mean way up here." the Small man asked.

"I don't reckon they would, but quit ye worrin'. I'm tired of hearin' it."

The Small man turned back to his gazing into the fire. Then he asked,

"Reckon we can git across the county tomorrow?"

"We better. We can git over the state line, I figure, by sometime during the day. Can't be hitchin' no rides, though."

"Might can steal a car if we lucky," the Small man said without much hope in his voice.

"Might can, but goddamnit we'd be a heap better off if ye hadn't done it. I don't reckon they coulda pinned that one over in Troy on us, but they sure goin' connect with this here one now. You and that damn ice pick of yourn."

"Tell you the truth, I kinda wished I hadn't done it. Not like I did. That girl worn't nothing but trouble from the start. A perdy thing, though."

"She weren't too bad. No point in killin' her, way I see it."

"If she jis' hadn't kept laughin' at me. Calling me Stubby."

"Well, you are right stubby."

"You know good as me that worn't what she was talkin' about. After you finished with her she didn't want no part of me. I didn't care much about that. I coulda done what I wanted with her, but she didn't have to go and make fun of me. Jis kept laughin' and gigglin' calling me Stubby. Over and over. I didn't have to listen to that. You wouldn't have."

"She didn't call me Shorty" the Big man chuckled.

"I don't like people makin' fun of me. I ain't puttin' up with it."

"She won't do it no more, that's for sure. Not after you stuck her a dozen time with that ice pick. No siree, I reckon she won't."

"I jis' ain't goin' to listen to nobody makin' fun of me. Least not no girl," declared the Small man. Then, "I sure need me a damn drank." He wiped his dry lips with the back of his hand and began raking up the pines needles around him When he had a pile, he spread them out thickly for his bed. He lay down and stretched out by the fire. The other man continued to gaze hypnotically into it, his eyes cold and open. It was late and there were no more sounds from the distant highway. Finally, he sat up, leaning away from the tree.

"You asleep yet?"

"Naw, this ground's hard. Pine needles ain't helpin' much. Dammit it, wish I had me a drank."

"Look, I been sittin' here thinkin'. Ye stuck that feller over in Wofford County and now this here girl. When they find her, I mean if they do, they goin' to know they's connected. Any way you cut it. Both killed with a ice pick."

"We jis' gotta run, that's all. I got kin up in Munro County. They won't never find us up in one of them hollers. My kin'll look after us."

"Maybe, but something else is troublin' *me* about it."

"What?" asked the Small man as he half raised himself on one elbow.

"You remember that boy we seen fishing in the creek? The little smart-ass one?"

"Yeah. She'd had him too if she coulda. Seen the way she was a lookin' at him?"

"Well, if we seen him then he seen us. He knows what we look like. He got a real good look at me. I don't reckon none of them cops over in Troy ever knew what we looked like, but this here young'un does for sure"

"Yeah, may be, but I don't see what we can do about it. We jis' gotta run."

"He could finger us."

"Ain't no use worryin' about it now. We hid her perdy good. Dogs or bears'll find her if they ain't already. She's bound to be a rottin'."

"Shouldn't be too hard to find the kid. Said he lived on a river. You heard him say it, didn't ye?" asked the Big man, ignoring the comments of the other.

"I reckon I heard him, but I was perdy drunk and tryin' git my hands in that girl's britches. I worn't payin' too much attention to the Boy."

"I was, and he said the river so I reckon it can't be far from here. I wish we know'd more about these parts."

"The girl coulda helped us."

"Well, yeah, but if she was here then we wouldn't need to go a lookin' for no kid, now would we?"

"I reckon not," responded the Small man blandly. "Ye aimin' to try and find him and kill him? Ye ain't, are you?"

"We got to, the way I see it."

"Damn, I don't know. I ain't never killed a young'un before."

"And you ain't goin' kill this one neither. Not with no ice pick. We find him and I'll take care of it. That way, won't be no connection."

"All right."

The Small man lay back down. With his head in the crook of an arm, he fell into a fitful sleep. The Big man leaned back against the dead tree and stared into the dying fire.

CHAPTER 4

The office, its drab green walls faded and peeling, was cramped and hot. The air- conditioning unit in the window hummed and rattled off and on, but produced little, if any, cool air. The ceiling fan beat impotently above the Deputy who leaned back in the swivel chair, his booted feet crossed at the ankles and resting on the desk. He gazed out the window to his left, preoccupied. He didn't bother to turn and look toward the door as it banged open.

"Damn, it's hot as hell in here!" exclaimed the thin wiry man as he stepped into the room. He was uniformed same as the Deputy. "That AC ain't doing a thing, is it?"

"Not much," said the Deputy. "What's up?"

"Nothing, I was just fixing to call in an order to the Tic-Toc for some lunch. I'll walk over there and pick it up. You want anything?"

"Yeah, get me a sweet tea. No lemon."

"Nothing to eat?"

"Just sweet tea."

The diminutive policeman turned to leave, but stopped at the door.

"Say, did you find out anything over in Corinth the other day?"

"Didn't make it to Corinth. Not yet, anyhow. Went on up the road though. Up near the crime scene."

"Learn anything?"

"Not much. Had a good hotdog, though."

"Damn, that's a shame. Going all way over there for nothing but a hot dog. No kind of lead or nothing?"

"Well, not much of one. Old gal at a store other side of Russellville, up there near the turn off to Sadler's Creek, said a boy came in that day. Never seen him before, she said. That's about it."

"Might be a suspect you think?"

"Nah, don't think so. Just a young'un going fishing. I'm thinking maybe he could have seen something, but who knows?" said the Deputy, his tone somewhat dispirited.

"You didn't go talk to him?"

"Don't know who he is, much less where he is. Like I said, the woman at the store didn't know him."

"Thought of maybe doing some police work?" the man smirked good naturedly.

"Why don't you go on and get you some lunch and stop being a wise-ass."

"Just—I don't know—it ain't like you to give up on a thing. Not something like this."

"Who said anything about giving up on it? I'll find the bastard with the ice pick. Don't you worry yourself none about that."

"You going to talk with the boys in over in Corinth?"

"I reckon so," said the Deputy.

"They might know more than what's been in the paper. I'd go on over there and at least see what they got to allow. I mean, if it was me, that's what I'd do."

"Yeah, at some point I reckon I will. But I'm going to try and find that boy first."

"How you going to that? Not knowing his name. Storekeeper didn't know him. So what now?"

"Like you said, do a little police work."

"Well, it's for sure he lives somewhere."

"I'm waiting on that sweet tea," said the Deputy as he returned to his window-gazing and thoughts.

Up until they found the girl over in McBee County he had figured the killer, or killers, was long gone. There was little to go on and the trail had grown cold—until now. He was still around. Probably hiding out or holed up someplace waiting for the chance to run. But the deputy just couldn't see how the girl's murder made any sense. Up in the woods, naked and half buried, covered with dead leaves and rotten pine limbs. At least Cecil had been robbed. Pushed an ice pick into the back of his neck right into his brain. Like a push cushion. Maybe he was just an animal. It might be as simple as that. A psycho. Mean, and a little crafty maybe, but likely not real smart. I'd rather have them mean than smart any day, he thought.

Finally, the deputy stood up and put on his hat, adjusting it by the faint reflection in the window. As he walked around the desk and reached for the door knob the door flew open, barely missing his face.

"Here's your tea," the other deputy said as he placed a large Styrofoam cup on the desk. A thick slice of lemon was slit and hugged the rim of the cup.

"I said no lemon."

"Damn, you did, didn't you? I plain forgot."

"I reckon that new waitress over at the Tic-Toc must have distracted you."

"Nah, it wasn't that. I just forgot."

"Yeah, right. If I'd wanted lemonade, I'd have ordered lemonade. Ever seen me take lemon with my tea?"

"No, can't say as I have."

The Deputy removed the lemon slice and dropped it into the wastebasket beside the desk. He took a sip of the ice tea and checked his watch.

"You headed out?"

"Thought I'd ride back over to McBee County and talk to that store woman again. She's about the only lead I got right now, if you can call it that."

"Going get you a hotdog, I'll bet."

"I might. None of your concern if I do. I'm just thinking she might know more than she told me. You never get it all the first time around. Maybe something's turned up."

"Them McBee County boys ain't likely going to like it much, you poking around their jurisdiction."

"Don't worry about it. I'm working a case, too." He took another sip of the tea and placed the cup back on the desk. "Ain't you got something to do?"

"I do, for sure. Soon as I finish my eating my lunch I'm going down to the school crossing. There's been complaints about speeders."

"I'll be back directly," mumbled the Deputy.

He slowed the cruiser as he approached the turnoff to Russellville, but he did not make the turn. On impulse, he decided to drive on down to Corinth and talk with the boys there. It wouldn't hurt to share what little information he had and maybe they would do the same. Anyway, it was the right thing to do. What a sheriff would be expected to do.

Most of the people in and around Corinth, the natives at least, considered Troy and the rest of Wofford County to be a little behind the times, not quite what they called progressive. And they were pretty much right. During most of the twentieth century both McBee and Wofford Counties, like the rest of the Southeast, had depended on the cotton mills. Then foreign countries began buying up all the old looms and by the time Bill Clinton and the Bushes were through, the mills and the jobs they provided were gone—gone to places like Mexico, India, and particularly China. The industry in the South became a pathetic shell of what it once had been.

But McBee County, and particularly the city of Corinth, had survived and prospered as new, more sophisticated manufacturing and high-tech companies moved in. New money and new wealth. Companies that made things Americans are good at making, like turbines, tires, and software. The old, low-paying cotton mill jobs were gone, replaced by higher paying ones, by jobs that required more education, more training. So Corinth began to see itself as a gleaming jewel in the crown of the New South. Troy and the rest of Wofford County were the red-headed stepchildren—provincial, rural, and more than a little behind the times. As a police officer in Wofford County, he liked it slow. That's why he had moved there years ago, after his discharge. But he was the acting-Sheriff now, at least for a while, and he would act like it.

He slowed the patrol car as he approached the high overpass on the new, divided four lane leading into Corinth. Off to his left were new apartments and office buildings going up. Construction seemed to be everywhere, as huge cranes effortlessly lifted and lowered gray, steel girders into place. The high-rise buildings seemed to almost be growing out of the concrete and asphalt-layered earth below.

But off to his right was West Corinth. The cotton mills, now all silent and empty, lay out before him, scattered like giant red-brick coffins containing no bodies, but waiting for burial just the same. Each with its rusting water tower and guarded over by a tall, cold, smoke stack of the same red brick—eerie reminders of a faded past that now seemed far away and unreal. The row upon row of dilapidated mill houses, identical from this distance, looked bleak and shabby, the inhabitants now mostly black or Hispanic, and all poor. This had become the mostly forgotten "bad side" of town. He had grown up here.

He shook off the almost dreamy trance of the dreary panorama and the memories that came with it. He pressed the accelerator and sped through a traffic light, its yellow eye giving him a portent wink.

The side trip to Corinth turned out to be a waste of time. The McBee County sheriff was entertaining some politician up from Columbia, and couldn't—or wouldn't—see him. After waiting a good thirty minutes, he was shown in to one of the assistants' office. The young officer was sitting behind a polished oak desk and did not rise to greet the older deputy. Damn, he looks right out of the academy, he thought. College kid. Looks more like a branch manager of a bank than a cop, what with the suit and all.

The young officer was patronizing and seemed bored with the meeting. He sat at his desk and pretended to be listening to the deputy, but was betrayed by the frequent glances at his gold wrist watch. Although unspoken, the Deputy knew there would be no assistance from the McBee sheriff or any of his people. Besides, the McBee police didn't seem to have made much progress in the case or have any new information, at least any they were willing to share. There just didn't seem to be much interest. Hard to get excited about the murder of a drunk slut up in the hills above Russellville, the young Corinth policeman had smirked. The Deputy didn't much care about the murder either except for the link it had with the killing in his own county.

"We appreciate your stopping by, deputy. You go right ahead and snoop around all you want to, but I assure you we'll apprehend the perpetrator. That's for sure. But you go right ahead." Perpetrator. Yep, right out of the academy, degree and all. And he could *snoop* around, that's what he'd said—*snoop around*. He was assured that they would let him know if something turned up, as he was quickly ushered from the office.

As he rounded the bend he saw the now-familiar store up ahead. The woman was outside listlessly picking up litter near the door. He eased the patrol car onto the dirt yard, just off the road. She looked up, shading her eyes with her hand as he got out of the car.

"Well, well, well," she said. "I figured I'd see you again."

"Yeah, why's that?"

"Cause you like my hotdogs." She laughed hoarsely and began to cough.

"You all right?"

"I reckon so. Them cheap cigarettes 'bout to kill me."

"Don't smoke them then."

She pulled a wrinkled pack of cigarettes from the pocket of her jeans, took one out and lit it. When she exhaled, the bluish smoke hung briefly in the still, hot air.

"I was just kidding about the hotdogs, but I figure I know why you're back up here."

The deputy walked around to the passenger side of his car and leaned against the hood, his hat pushed back from his perspiring forehead.

"That so?"

"It's about that girl that was killed, ain't it? You never said for sure, I mean when you was here before."

"Might be. What if it is?"

"I knowed it. They ain't found who done it and I'm bettin' you ain't got a clue."

"You pretty much got that right. I just wanted to talk with you again. See if we overlooked anything or maybe something you forgot.

"I ain't forgot nothin'. My mind's a good as yourn."

"We all forget things," said the deputy.

"Come on inside and get out of the sun. I got my fans going."

He followed her inside the store. She resumed her usual perch on the stool behind the counter. He walked back to the drink box and pulled a Tom's Orange from the icy water. He leaned against the edge of the picnic table nearest the counter, facing her.

"I'd like to go over it again. I mean when the boy came in that morning. You said he was going fishing, I believe. You did say that, didn't you?"

"Yep, that's what I said."

"And about how old did you say he was?"

"Aw, I don't know. Thirteen or fourteen, no more than that."

"Can you describe him?"

"What do you mean?"

"You know, what did he look like?"

"Like I done told you, he was a skinny kid. His hair was cut short, like a crew-cut. Light headed, you know, blondish."

"How about his eyes, can you recall what color they were?"

"No," she sighed, with a degree of exasperation.

"About how tall?"

"I don't know. Not tall for his age. Not short neither. A little shorter than me. 'Bout five foot, I'd say. Just a plain looking kid."

"Tell me again what he was wearing," said the Deputy after taking a long draw from the bottle of orange soda.

"Well, I didn't take no picture of him, but far as I can remember he had on a white tee shirt, or maybe it was gray. I ain't sure. Light colored though. I noticed his blue jeans though. One of the knees had a hole in it."

"And you ain't seen him before or since, that right?"

"That's right, sheriff."

"Deputy, acting sheriff."

"Whatever. I wish I could help you, but I can't. Simple as that. He could have been anybody's kid. Did kind of look like one of them Reddens though, come to think of it. But that ain't likely." The woman lit a fresh cigarette from the one she was smoking.

"Redden? Who's that?"

"Aw, I'm just talkin'. I went to high school with a bunch of 'em. Reddens, I'm talkin' about. They was a pretty rough bunch, if you know what I mean. Poor as Job's turkey. I mean we all was poor, but not like them."

"Where was this?"

"High school."

"What high school?"

"Over at Russellville. That's where I growed up at. They all lived down somewhere on the river. We didn't have much to do with 'em. Like I said, they was a rough bunch. Might have been loggers or something. I don't know for sure."

"Well, that ain't much to go on," said the Deputy, placing the empty bottle on the table.

"I never said it was, now did I?"

"No, I reckon you didn't."

"You want me to fix you a hotdog?"

"No, I best be getting on," he moved to the counter to pay for the soda. "By the way, has the McBee County police been back up here? Have you seen them?

"No, just that one time I told you about. Hell, they ain't goin' waste their time on that girl. Can't say as I blame 'em?"

"I reckon not," he said.

"Then why you so interested in all this?"

"Might be connected to something over in my neck of the woods. Sounds like the same killer."

"They say he used a ice pick on her. That right?"

"Don't know that it was a *he,* but likely is. I appreciate you talking with me again. Here's a department card. That number there on it is my office. If you see or hear anything that you think I might be interested in, I'd be much obliged if you'd call me. Collect is okay."

"Reckon I can afford a phone call to the next county, Mr. Deputy Sheriff." She crushed the cigarette butt in the glass ashtray on the counter.

"Didn't mean nothing by it. Thanks anyway."

She watched as he walked out the door and got into the patrol car. He turned onto the black top and sped away back toward Russellville. Suddenly, she remembered the two men, reprobates she had called them to herself, who had stopped in the store for beer that day, asking stupid questions, interested in where the river was. Probably ought to call the Deputy and tell him, she thought. Maybe she would, but it seemed kind of silly to her the more she thought about. Just be wasting his time. She slipped his card into the back pocket of her jeans.

CHAPTER 5

From her stool that day she had watched the two men approach the store from the edge of the woods across the county road. They stopped at the rusting gas pumps and sat down on the concrete base facing the road, their backs to her, shuffling their feet in loose gravel.

Now that's a mangy looking pair, she thought as she flicked ashes from her cigarette onto the floor. Wonder what the hell they're up to.

A car sped by and the Big man lowered his head and the other looked back over his shoulder toward the store. He spotted the water spigot and then made his way over to it once the automobile was out of sight. Cupping his hands, he splashed water on his face. It ran down his neck in dirty streaks. He knelt beside the spigot and drank. After wiping his face with a rag from his pocket he stood and strode into the store, leaving his seedy companion sitting at the old pumps.

"Howdy," he said, the screen door slamming hard behind him.

"What can I do for you?"

"Thought we might git us a couple of cold beers."

"I got beer. You got money?"

"Enough for two beers, I reckon."

"Beer's in that red cooler over yonder with all the other drinks. Help yourself."

He went back to the cooler and pulled two cans of beer from the icy water. He sat them, dripping, on the counter and reached to pull the pop-top.

"Can't drink 'em in here or on the premises. I ain't got no license." Only my regulars can drink on the premise, she started to say, but thought better of it. "You want a bag?"

"Naw, I don't need no bag. How much?"

"Four dollars."

He fumbled in his pocket and withdrew several dollar bills, all grimy and wrinkled.

"These here apples for sale?" he asked, glancing at the small basket on the counter.

"I reckon they are or I wouldn't have 'em on the counter. Fifty-cents apiece."

"Gimme two." He placed five of the crumpled bills on the wet counter.

"Anything else?" she asked, hoping there wasn't. She wanted these two off her property. She'd seen enough trouble in her life to recognize it in these two.

"I reckon you *can* put the beers in a sack since we gotta drink 'em walkin'."

She looked at him hard, pursed her lips, and pulled two small paper bags from underneath the counter and placed a can of beer in each. She pushed the bags across the counter to him. He shoved the apples into his trouser pockets. He picked up the bags and walked toward the door.

"Say, ain't there a river around here somewhere?" he asked, stopping and turning backed to the woman.

"There's Sadler's Creek up that dirt road there," she said.

"Naw, I ain't talkin' about no creek. I mean a real river."

"What do you want to know that for?"

"Heard that might be a nice river around here. Might want to go catfishing sometime, that's all."

"Nearest river is down yonder south of Russellville, the Cootawachee," she pointed vaguely out down the county road.

"That a right fer piece?" he asked, squinting, his eyes dark pools behind the slits of the lids.

"Right far," was all she offered.

"Might ye know anybody lives down on the river?" he asked.

Annoyed, she leaned toward him, her forearms on the counter. "Look, mister, I don't know who you are or what you're lookin' for, but I can't help you. You and your buddy out there best be movin' along. I ain't answerin' no more of your questions."

"All right," he said, his thin lips in a tight smile. "I 'preciate it." He turned and left the store.

The woman watched the man pass a bagged beer to his companion still sitting at the old gas pumps. He then stood and they both crossed the road onto the shoulder and headed south toward Russellville, sipping the beer, the damp paper bags twisted tightly around each can.

The store was barely out of sight behind them when they finished the beer and tossed the cans into the red clay gulley that ran just beyond the narrow shoulder of the road.

"What's that there bulgin' in yer pockets?"

"Apples."

"Gimme one of 'em. I'm 'bout starved."

The Big man pulled both apples from his pocket. He handed him one of them to his crony and chomped down hard on the other. They quickly devoured the apples.

"Sure wish I had a cigarette."

"Well, you don't so shut up about it."

"You find anything out back there at the store?"

"Not much. Talked to the old hag runnin' the place. She weren't none too friendly neither."

"What'd she allow?"

"Said they's a river down south of Russellville."

"Damn, Munro County's back the other way. We jis' need to git out of here. Forgit the young'un. He won't make no connection with us. Just a dumb kid."

"I ain't forgittin' nothin'." They walked on.

"Did she say anything about knowin' the boy?"

"Didn't ask her, not directly. She was a bitch."

"I bet she'd told me after I got done with her."

"Shut up," said the Big man. They walked on.

The river began from a deep spring and was fed by a series of clear, pristine streams high in the mountains in the northeastern part of the county near the state line. As it widened and coursed south, red mud flowed into it from deep gullies—rain-chiseled gashes in the bare earth—left by the loggers when the forest was clear-cut decades before. Just north of Russellville, on the river, there had once been a plant for bleaching cloth. For years, waste—toxic and fetid—was dumped routinely and unconscionably into it. The cotton mills, those with dye houses, down near Corinth made further contributions to the death of the river with unbridled discharge of their sludge into it. Some life remained in the depths of the river, some forms of algae, shellcrackers, and inedible catfish. At least the State environmental people *advised* folks not catch and eat them. By the time it flowed a mile south of Russellville, the river was a broad, slow moving band of smelly, muddy water.

CHAPTER 6

The road was only recently tarred and graveled, and looked as forlorn and abject as the men on the county chain gang that had paved it. It would be a long time before there would be any more work to the road. It led to nowhere and the few people who used it—mainly those who lived on it—weren't much interested in its condition one way or the other. It forked off the highway at the bend of a sharp curve and could be easily missed even if a person was actually looking for it, which was unlikely. A faded green sign, held by a single bolt in one corner, dangled from a rusting angle-iron post. *River Road*, it read.

The two men, hunched and shadowy even in the glaring sun, shuffled languidly along the edge of the highway. With the occasional approaching vehicle, with heads down and eyes averted, they moved to the shoulder and continued walking. When it passed, the Small man always looked back to see if it slowed or might be stopping. None had.

"Looky yonder at that sign. Can ye read it from here?"

"No," replied the Big man as he quickened his pace. Within a few yards of the sign he stopped and squinted. "Says River Road."

"Reckon it's the one?"

"Come on," he said, ignoring the question, as he walked passed the sign and turned down onto the narrow tar and gravel road. The Small man followed him, almost running to catch up.

" 'Least they's some trees shadin' the road. Wish I had another one of them cold beers."

"Shut up."

They walked on in silence along the road, but soon the sparse shade again gave way to the white sun. The land on both sides of the road was clear-cut and was now a desolate wasteland of stumps, scrubby pines, and red-gashed gullies. They had passed no houses nor met any cars. In the simmering stillness they might have been the only living things on the planet. They walked on in silence except for their heavy breathing and the gravel-crunch of their shoes on the rough pavement. Those were the only sounds, and the stench of their sweat the only smell.

Finally, the road curved and slanted slightly more downward, into a canopy of water oaks and tall hickories. There was shade and an inexplicable sense of a stale dampness, but the summer silence hung in the thick, hot air. The Big man increased his pace.

"What's ye hurry?"

"Up ahead yonder's a mail box."

"I don't see no mailbox," the Small man dully responded.

The Big man walked on briskly, then slowed his pace as he approached the mail box and stood looking at it as his crony, almost gasping, caught up with him. The faded, black hand-lettering on the metal mail box was ragged and uneven, like a child just learning to write might have scribbled.

"What's it say?"

"*Redden,*" said the Big man.

Beside the mail box was a dirt path that wound and sloped sharply down from the road. The path gave way to a wide yard, also dirt, and a small unpainted house beyond it. On the narrow porch of the house sat an old man on a couch, his stubbled chin resting on his chest. His snoring was soft and regular. A mongrel dog, large and brown, lay dozing in the shade just beneath the porch.

"They's a house down there," said the Small man.

"I see it. Old man on the porch. Let's go down there and see what he's got to allow."

"Reckon we ort to?"

"What are you talkin' about?"

"You don't reckon he'd know nothing, ye know, like what's been going on and all. I don't want to take no chances."

"Stuck way back down in here? He won't know nothing. Except who that boy might be. Come on."

"I don't like it."

"Shut up."

As the two figures started down the path the dog woke. It slid out effortlessly from underneath the porch and took a low, defensive stance in the yard, growling ferociously. The two men trudging down the path stopped.

"When dogs growl like that they mean business. I don't like it when a dog don't bark," said the Small man. The other man stooped and picked up a thick stick lying beside the path.

"This here stick ought to take care of him if he don't back off."

The dog's movement and growling woke the old man and he sat up slowly and leaned forward as he looked up toward the path. He wiped a dried tobacco stain from the corner of his mouth with the knuckles of a fist. As the two men advanced slowly, a thin line of hair on the dog's back bristled and the growl became more guttural. They stopped at the edge of the yard. The old man stood up slowly with great effort, almost painfully, and leaned against the post near the porch steps. He didn't speak. He dug a hand into the right pocket his overalls and lightly fingered the revolver.

"Howdy," said the Big man.

"What can I do fer y'uns?" asked the old man after a long moment.

"Hot, ain't it. I mean for this late?"

"Whatcha want?" The dog had not moved, still growling.

"We don't want nothin'. Maybe a drink of water if you could spare it."

"I'll give you some water, but you best not come in the yard. I can't do much with ole Butch there when it comes to strangers," the old man said, almost with a chuckle. "Y'all just wait right there where you are. I'll be back directly." The two men on the path looked at each other, but did not move into the yard.

The old man went into the house and returned with two small Mason jars of water. He walked across the yard, past the dog, and gave one to each of the two men. They gulped down the water immediately and handed the empty jars back to the old man.

"You won't be needing that there stick, feller," said the old man. The Big man tossed it into the weeds beside the path. "Y'all lost? Don't get many people down River Road, not hoofing it, anyway."

"Damned car broke down a ways back, up on the highway. I got some distant kin lives around here somewhere. Don't know where exactly, but I think it's somewheres down here on the river."

"Is that a fact?"

"I reckon it is."

"What's their name?" asked the old man.

"Well, you might know 'em. Got a boy. A skinny runt. I reckon he'd be near 'bout thirteen by now," said the Big man, ignoring the old man's question.

"Got no name, though?"

"Well, they's kin all right. Jis' fer kin. I reckon you could say."

"Hmm," said the old man, scratching his grizzled chin with dirty finger nails. "They's a heavy-set gal lives down the road there apiece. Don't know much about her 'cept I seen a young'un around there lately. Skinny boy, like you said. Seen him fishing on the river a couple of times. Just seemed he showed up there one day, I mean down at this gal's place. I don't reckon he's hers."

"Say it's on down the road a ways?"

"About half a mile, I'd say. It's an old, blue house trailer. Sets way back off the road down by the river. Rents it, I reckon, but I don't really know or give a damn.

"We much obliged, mister. Thank ye for the water, too."

"Kin, you say?"

"Fer kin, I said."

"I reckon you boys better head on out. Looks like ole Butch there's getting a mite impatient," said the old man. He shifted both Mason jars to his left hand and slipped his right back into in his overalls pocket. "I don't see much point in y'all coming 'round here again."

"I reckon we won't, at that," said the Big man. He stood for a moment, staring at the old man like he might have something else to say to him. The old man stared back at him, and then spat a long stream of tobacco juice onto the hard, sunbaked ground near where the two men stood.

"Come on, let's go," said the Small man nervously, and both of them turned and walked heavily back up the hill toward the road. The old man didn't take his fingers off the pistol until they were out of sight.

CHAPTER 7

The two men left the old man standing in his yard with the growling dog and the pistol in his pocket. They walked down the road, passing several more unpainted clapboard shacks and trailers, several with the name *Redden* inscribed in varying degrees of legibility on roadside mailboxes. Up ahead the road descended sharply and appeared to dead end into a stand of poplar trees. But down off to their left sat an old blue house trailer perched precariously on cinder blocks stacked at each corner. The murky river, wide and slow-moving, ran along the shaded, damp bank behind and just below the low bluff on which the trailer rested, ugly and squat.

"Reckon that's it?" asked the Small man.

"Perdy much it has to be. Road's about run out. It's a beat-up old blue house trailer, ain't it?"

"Hit don't look so bad to me. I lived in worse."

"Come on, let's git down there," said the Big man. "Follow this here gully."

The ground slanted abruptly from the road down to the trailer and the river bank. The two men cursed as they tried to navigate the red-clay gullies and as thick, low briary vines grabbed the rough cloth of their trouser legs. The Big man stumbled on a pine stump and fell into a clump of briars. The other attempted to help him to his feet, but he pushed him away and cursed him. His huge hands were scratched and bled from the pricks, the blood mixing with the sweat and grime of his skin. He pushed himself up off the ground, wiping his torn hand across the front of his shirt, and spat. He moved on.

They finally got to the dirt yard of the trailer. The steps to the front door were unevenly stacked cinder blocks. The narrow, aluminum front door was shut. Across the yard a wide board rested on two large, river rocks making a low, rough bench.

"Whew, I got to sit me down a spell. 'Bout killed myself coming down that hill. Can't hardly catch my breath." The Small man slumped down on the bench, his head down with his elbows on his knees. The Big man looked absentmindedly at his open palms, scratched and still bleeding, and then across the yard to the door of the trailer. Then there beside the door, leaning against the trailer, he saw it. Something he thought he recognized. He grinned and forgot about his shredded hands.

"Look over there beside the door," he said, keeping his eyes focused on the object. His seated, breathless crony did not look up. The Big man strode over to the trailer. "Well, looky, here won't ye. I reckon we done found us a fisherman."

He reached and grasped the rod with the spinning reel attached. He examined it closely and with a dirt-encrusted fingernail flicked off a dry chip of the fiberglass, an old South Bend. The Small man had finally taken notice and ambled over to take a look.

"A rod and reel. I reckon near everybody on the river has a rod and real, or a cane pole," he said when he saw what the Big man held in his hands.

"May be, but this one here's different."

"Looks 'bout shot to me."

"I believe it's the one the boy was carryin'. The boy we seen up on that creek."

"Could be. I didn't pay much attention to it at the time."

"You was too drunk and pawing that gal."

"I weren't no drunker than you was, I don't reckon."

"I was drunk, but not too drunk. I aim to see things even when I'm drinkin'. This here is his rig." He placed the rod and reel back against the side of the trailer and strode over to the bench and sat down.

"What you reckon we ort to do now?" asked the Small man.

"Let me think a minute. When we was standing over there beside the door did you hear anything?"

"No, I didn't hear nothing."

"Well, I did. The TV's playin' in there. I heard it clear."

"You reckon somebody's here."

"I reckon so."

Half dozing, she blinked rapidly and then opened her eyes, unsure of what had woken her. There was something, not a natural noise. There was tapping on the front door. Then silence and she waited. When it came again she slowly pushed herself up from the chair with great effort. She switched off the television and shuffled to the door. When the door opened, the Small man backed down off the steps and stood in the dirt yard. He quickly glanced back at the other man sitting on the bench, giggled stupidly, and then looked up at the woman who filled the doorway.

"What do you want, bangin' on my door like that?" she drawled, her speech slightly slurred from the interrupted nap. "What you doin' way down here bangin' on doors for anyway?" she said. "You 'bout scared the life out of me. Y'all go on get out of here!"

"Why, we didn't mean to bother you none. Jis need to use your telephone, if it ain't too much bother to you. That's right, we jis need to use yer phone. Ye see, our old car broke down up yonder on the highway. We near broke, but if can use your telephone, ye see, I can call my brother-in-law to come git us."

"I ain't got no telephone," she said. She then looked beyond him at the man sitting on the bench. He ain't half bad looking, she thought. A lot better than this squirrely runt. "Your buddy over there, cat got his tongue?"

"Naw, he's all right."

The Big man stood up and sauntered across the yard, his hands in his pockets, he stood next to the other in the dirt.

"I can talk, all right," he said, rubbing his chin and slowly, perusing the yard and the trailer before looking up directly at her. "Perdy nice place ye got here. With the river and all."

"It's quiet," she said, her tone softening.

"Yeah, real nice and quiet. I like that, too. Seeing is ye ain't got no phone maybe we could jis rest here a spell before we walk back up to the highway. That's a right steep bank we got to climb back up."

"I guess I got no problem with you restin' here a while. It's hot as hell, I can tell you that much."

The Big man nudged the other and motioned with his head back toward the bench. They both returned to the bench and sat down. The Small man had picked up a stick and began scratching in the dirt with it. The other man leaned over, his forearms resting on his knees. He had not taken his eyes off the woman.

"This here shade is fine, but the air's mighty still. Ain't nary a breeze a-stir," he said.

"Dog days, I reckon," offered the woman as she plopped down clumsily in the door way, her feet resting on a cinder block step. She pulled a pack of cigarettes from the waistband of the sweat pants which had been raggedly cut off just above her knees. She withdrew a cigarette and the man watched her light it. "Things is mighty dry, too. Cloudin' up, though. Might get some rain this evenin'." She stuffed the pack back into her pants waist.

"I ain't much for rain," he said.

"Well, I reckon you ain't no farmer, then," she chuckled and took a long drag on the cigarette.

"Nope, too much work to suit me and too little to show for it most of the time," he said with a sinister grin. "Say, like my partner here said, we plumb near broke and run out of smokes a ways back. Could you spare us one of them cigarettes?" He stood up and slowly took a few steps toward the woman.

With this, the Small man glanced up quickly. He quit scratching in the dirt with the stick and strode over to where his companion was standing. He nervously pinched his lower lip, rolling it back and forth between his thumb and forefinger.

"Sure would be obliged for a smoke," he added.

"Sure, why not?" said the woman. The men did not move. "Well, I sure as hell ain't goin' to bring 'em to you."

The Big man elbowed his crony sharply and motioned for him to step over and get the cigarettes, which he did. The woman again retrieved the pack from her waist band and handed it to him. The cellophane glistened with the woman's sweat. He withdrew two cigarettes from the pack and quickly placed one in his mouth. He looked up at the woman.

"Need a light, too?" she asked.

"I reckon I do."

"Looks like you boys ain't got nothing but the habit," she smirked and handed him a book of matches.

The air hung still and heavy over the yard as the two men sat on the bench smoking in silence. She lit another but did not take her eyes off them across the dirt expanse. The world was stilled by the heat and the only recompense seemed to be the silence. Nothing stirred, the woods beyond the trailer were dark, the tree tops motionless, the river seemed motionless and solid, not water at all.

Finally, the Big man took a final draw and crushed the butt in the dirt between his feet. He glanced at the rod and reel still leaning against the trailer.

"I reckon you do a lot of fishing, what with a big ole river flowin' jis back of where you live."

"Not much. I ain't much of for fishing. I *do* like to eat 'em, though, if they fried fresh."

"Well, I jis seen yer pole there against the trailer and figured..."

"That old rod and reel? That's my nephew's. He fancies hisself as some kind of fish catcher, I reckon. He ain't much of one neither, but he does manage to bring in some perdy good catfish on occasion."

"I see. I reckon he fishes when he comes to visit you?"

"Naw, I ain't that lucky. Point is, he stays with me now. Damn laziest young'un you ever seen. Wouldn't work in a pie factory."

"Then he's likely inside nappin', I reckon."

"He would be if he could. Naw, I sent him to school today. Done layed out too much. Wouldn't go atall if I didn't make him."

"A young'un, ye say?"

"That's right. Just a scrawny kid. He's—was—my sister's. Daddy's in jail. On the chain gang over in Wofford County. I'm all the kin he's got that's worth a damn. His mama got the cancer and died. Young, too."

"Likely ain't no barrel of fun raisin' a young'un like that."

"No, it ain't."

"Say he likes to fish in that there river?"

"Yep, most of the time."

"Jis this river?"

"Yeah, 'til here lately anyhow. Seems catfish ain't good enough for him no more. Got a wild hair and took up trout fishing. That's what he calls it, anyway. Says he has to catch 'em in real clean water. With Niblet corn of all things. You never heard such crap."

"I heard of trout fishing. I don't reckon they none in this here river?"

"Reckon not. He goes up there in them hills somewhere above Russellville. Some creek."

"Well, ain't that something. Him with that big ole river in his own backyard. Don't make no sense, now does it?"

"None that I can see. Like I said, ain't much to him. But he's my sister's boy and all. You know how it is."

"Yeah, kin's kin."

During the exchange with the woman the Small man said nothing, but returned to his scratching the dirt with the stick. But he had been listening, and closely. At first, it hadn't seemed likely that they would find the boy, but maybe they had after all. They would just have to wait and it shouldn't be long. I need to get out of here, he thought, and get on up to Munro County.

"Well, it's a shame a good lookin' woman like you got to be saddled with a snot-nosed kid, just the same."

"Why, ain't you the charmer. The boy ain't nothing. Jis' gets in the way sometimes, that's all."

"Sounds like ye might have a feller. Likely cuts into yer socializin'. I mean you a perdy good lookin' gal. They must be comin' around. Men, I mean, sniffin' around. That's right, ain't I?" He didn't smile nor did she.

"I got no beau if that what you're talkin' about. Not no more anyway." She sat up from her slouched position in the door way, her face flush. She lit another cigarette.

"Now, I can't believe that. A woman like you."

He's dirty, a little nasty even, but nothing a hot bath couldn't help, she thought, if it came to it. He seems right nice. She liked the way he spoke to her, his directness when he looked straight into her face. He didn't have to be smart.

He wiped the back of his hand across his lips.

"You the funny one, now ain't you. I don't go nowhere much anymore. All my kin's over 'round Troy. I ain't looking for no man, 'lest no live-in man. Y'all ain't nothing but trouble, all of y 'uns." She looked down at him where he stood, unsmiling. He shuffled his shoes in the dirt and glanced back at his partner.

"That why ye stuck way out here then? I mean, ye don't want nobody botherin' ye?"

"You ask too many questions." They were silent for a moment. She looked away, but he kept his eyes on her. Then she said, "Truth is, I got caught kitin' checks. Just tryin' to get by, you know. Magistrate over in Troy didn't quite see it that a-way, so I got the hell out of Dodge."

He shoved his hands into his pockets and strolled back to the bench, and sat down beside the Small man. She smoked, sweated, and watched them. In the hot silence the burden of conversation seemed too great. She squirmed a little and adjusted her position and leaned against the frame of the open doorway.

"Damn hot, ain't it. Seems like the whole world is fryin'," the Big man finally said, his voice thin and flat. The other man scratched in the dirt.

"Look," said the woman, "I know you boys got to be goin', but the heat's a'smotherin' out here. I might have a few cold beers in the ice box if you don't mind sittin' out here while you drink 'em. I don't think I know y'all good enough to ask you in. Besides, the kid'll be getting in from school directly."

The Big man gave a hard, squinted look at his companion. "A cold beer would go down real good 'bout now."

"I'll go see what I got." She grasped the frame of the door and pulled herself slowly erect, trying unsuccessfully to suppress a strained grunt. Her tee shirt was twisted and she quickly pulled it down over the white bulge of her flesh as she disappeared into the trailer.

"Cold beer sounds mighty satifyin' right now," said the Small man. The other man did not respond, but got up and walked to the end of the trailer and looked at the river below.

On the living room wall hung a mirror set in a gold, ornate plastic frame. The woman glanced at her image as she passed it. She smoothed down her hair with her small fleshy hands and pursed her lips and went into the kitchen. From the refrigerator she pulled three cans of Pabst Blue Ribbon from the plastic ringed six-pack.

She came back to the front door and looked over at the men on the bench. She hesitated and then walked out into the yard where they sat. She handed each a can of beer and pulled back the metal tab of the one she held for herself. She threw back a long swallow. The men did the same. The cans were quickly emptied. The Small man crushed his can and threw it into the weeds behind the bench. The Big man sat holding the empty can between his knees, his head down.

"There's three more in the ice box. We might as well drink them before you boys hit the road. Don't want nobody sayin' I ain't hospitable" she said. The Big man stood up.

"That's good beer, but I ain't much on holdin' it, if ye know what I mean. I got to go drain the dew off my lily." His laugh was hoarse and obscene. He started off toward the woods.

"Wait a minute there, big 'un. You ain't got to get behind no tree. I got a bathroom. I reckon I'd be all right for you to use it," she said.

"That's white of ye. I didn't want to appear pushy."

"Just go through the living room there. Bathroom's down the hall. Now don't you go messin' in my bedroom, you hear," she said with a thin, lewd laugh.

"No, I wouldn't go and do no such thing as that," he said.

"When you get through bring them other beers out here, will you?"

"Sure will," he said as he ambled up the cider block steps into the trailer.

"Your buddy there, he got a woman some place?" she asked the Small man.

"Naw, he ain't got no woman."

"Bet he could have one if he wanted to."

"Likely. He's a big'un."

She did not respond, but wiped the sweat from her forehead with the back of her hand. She then licked her lips with a flick of her tongue and adjusted the hem of her tee shirt.

He left the toilet and made his way down the narrow hallway into the kitchen. He took the beer from the refrigerator. In the living room, he placed the beer on the coffee table amid old soap opera magazines and an ashtray brimming over with broken and stale cigarette butts. He unplugged the television and pushed it away from the wall. Gripping the power cord with both hands he yanked it loose from the set. He then wound the cord into a tight coil, picked up the beer and went back out into the dirt yard.

"You must have really had to go," she said, almost giggling.

"Yeah, I did," he said, not smiling.

As he pulled the tab from a can, he extended it to her. He tossed a can to the man on the bench. "You can sit down there. He won't bite," he said her.

"All right, I believe I will at that. Hell, I ain't scared of him," she said, looking at the Small man.

They drank in silence, but sipped the beer slower this time. The Big man drained his can and dropped it in the yard. He then walked around behind the bench and looked up the gutted hill toward the road. The Aunt and the other man did not seem to notice.

"Yep, that's a mighty steep hill up to the road," said the Big man, finally.

"I reckon y'all could wait 'til this evenin' when it's cooler. You liable to have a sun stroke in this heat," she said, without turning toward him.

"That nephew of yours, he'll be coming in from school directly?"

"In a little while. He rides the school bus. Can't always predict exactly."

He let one end of the cord drop to his side and stood behind her. She felt him there and turned slightly on the bench. For a fatal moment she looked down at the dangling cord puzzled, with confusion on her face. Before she could speak or move, he grasped the loose end of the cord. In an instant he wrapped the garrote around her neck and pulled it tight. Then tighter. With dry guttural gasping sounds, she struggled and dug at the cord with both hands as it cut deeply into the flesh of her neck. He pulled her up close, her last breath hot, choking in his face. Her bulging eyes reflected his own as he ground his teeth and tightened the cord with a jerk. She suddenly went limp and her eyes were gone, only a lifeless milky whiteness where they had been. He maintained his hold for a moment longer and then let go of the cord. The woman fell to the ground and lay there in a grotesque, misshapen heap.

The Small man had watched the murder from where he sat on the bench. He had not moved nor had any change occurred to his expressionless face. The other man stood over the body, breathing heavily, standing erect, his feet wide apart. He rubbed spittle from each corner of his mouth with a knuckle of his hand.

"Bitch didn't go easy, did she?" said the Small man.

"They never do."

"With a ice pick they do."

"Shut up," said the Big man.

"Hand me that can. She didn't finish off her beer," said the Small man, reaching for the beer.

"Go to hell," grunted the Big man. He grabbed the can and sat down on the bench and gulped down the beer.

For a while both men sat on the bench smoking the woman's cigarette, glancing occasionally at the body lying in the dust of the yard before them. Neither had spoken.

"What ye reckon?" the Small man asked, finally breaking the silence.

"She said the boy ort to be comin' home directly. Don't expect he'll be much trouble, neither."

"When did you figure on killin' her?"

"She told us about the kid, didn't she?"

"Yep, I reckon she did. Came right out with it."

"I knowed right then. She seen us and seen us good. Weren't no way around it."

"All right. We take care of the Boy and then scram on up to Munro County. That's right, ain't it?"

"Yeah, that's right," answered the Big man, lighting the last of the cigarettes. "But we got to do something with her first."

"I was thinkin' about that, too. Got any idees?"

"The river, I reckon. It's deep and muddy and slow moving."

"Yeah, the river," repeated the Small man.

"Go on in the trailer and pull off three or four more cords. They's some lamps in there."

"All right."

"I'll drag her fat ass down to the river. You come on down there and tote two or three of them cinder blocks with you," the Big man said, standing up. Then with the cigarette dangling from the corner of his mouth, he reached down and grasped the dead woman by her ankles and dragged the body past the blue trailer down toward the river.

CHAPTER 8

With a scowl, the driver glanced up at the large, slanted mirror above his head as he turned on to River Road and his last stop of the day. It reflected the interior of the bus, allowing him see all the row of seats behind him. All were empty now except one. The kid sat at the very back, the last row. He always sat back there. It irritated the driver because he had to wait for him to come all the way up to the front of the bus to exit, and this his last stop. The kid just does it to spite me, he thought. Little piece of white trash.

The driver always passed the trailer where the Boy lived and drove to the end of the road where he turned the bus around. He drove back up River Road and let him out on the shoulder. The Boy didn't mind this, as he liked to be alone on the bus and be the last one off. It prolonged the time when he would have to see his aunt and listen to her, and endure the smell of burnt grease and stale cigarette smoke which permeated the trailer.

The bus slowed to a stop and he reached and lifted the backpack from the underneath the seat in front of him. He made his way slowly to the front of the bus and stepped down through the open door onto the hot road. Almost before he was off the bus, the door unfolded from itself and slammed shut. The bus pulled away, trailing a stream of black, diesel exhaust. He and the driver never spoke to each other.

He sauntered down the slanted hill from the road with the sure-footedness of youth, but as he approached the dirt yard he vaguely sensed something was awry, out of place or something. Then he noticed the steps at the front door.

Several of the cinder blocks were missing. He shrugged. Just his aunt doing something stupid with the blocks. He'd likely have to haul them back and fix the steps. He did not notice the scattered cigarette butts and beer cans in the dirt near the bench across the yard.

Once inside, he found the television set and the lamps upturned on the floor. The overhead fan rattled above, but there were no other sounds. He called for her, but no answer came. He waited and called out again. No answer. He walked down the hall to her room and slid back the flimsy pocket door. The bed was unmade, the dingy sheets in a wad at the foot and the pillows askew. Same as usual; he had never seen the bed made.

He went back into the living room and again surveyed the mess. What had happened, he wondered. Nothing good. Where would she have gone? It just didn't make any sense. He'd go look around in the woods maybe. As he turned to go into the kitchen he glanced out the back window which overlooked the river below. There he saw them. There were people down by the river. He squinted from the sunlight glaring off the aluminum frame of the window. Two men knelt, hunched over something on the bank.

Suddenly there seemed to be no air in the room. He couldn't breathe. He realized that it was the body of his aunt on the ground where the two men squatted. The cinder block steps. They lay on the ground beside her, one at her feet and another two near her head, at her throat. They seemed attached to her somehow. The men stood up and briefly looked down at the body. Then they stooped over and rolled it over into the muddy water. The cinder blocks were tied to her by the electrical cords. She sank immediately with hardly a ripple. The water instantly returned to its smooth, languid flow.

The Small man glanced back up at the trailer. The Boy instinctively sprang away from the window. Had they seen or heard him? He couldn't be sure. Maybe they had. He edged back toward the window just enough to see the river. The Small man and the Big man. Something was familiar about them. Something perverse and evil. He felt it. Suddenly he remembered. It was the two men with the girl that day up on Sadler's Creek. The same two smelly, drunk men. Strangely, he thought for an instant about the girl and wondered if she was with them now or nearby. But his attention quickly returned to the two men below. What were they doing here? It made no sense. They just stood there looking out at the river where they had dumped the body. What had happened? They had murdered her. That was for sure. They would be coming back up to the trailer. To where he was.

His thoughts raced and he realized the danger that he was in. His aunt was dead and there was nothing he could do about it now. His only emotion was fear, but he couldn't let it paralyze him. He turned from the window and glanced quickly around the room. Think, he told himself. They're going to kill me too, sure as hell they'll do it. But why? It made no sense to him. It didn't matter. Run, he knew that he must run.

He rushed into his room with his grimy yellow and black backpack, slamming it onto his bed. He grabbed it and tried to unzip it. Threads of worn, loose nylon caught in the zipper. He pulled on it harder, but the zipper was stuck. He tried to work it back and forth, but his fingers were moist with sweat and the zipper was difficult to grasp.

He wiped his palms down the legs of his jeans. With his fingers dry and with one violent yank, he yanked the zipper back and it gave. He pulled the zipper more carefully this time, holding the ragged strands of nylon away with his finger. Unzipped, he held the book bag up and shook it. Heavy text books crashed onto the carpeted floor with a dull thud. "Shit!" he said aloud. He then pulled some clothes—jeans and tee shirts—from the Small chest of drawers beside the bed. A pocket knife had also spilled from the book bag onto the floor. He quickly picked it up and jammed it into his pocket.

Dropping the backpack on the living room, he ran across the trailer back into his aunt's cluttered room. The air in the room was thick with the odor of stale cigarette smoke and liniment. He knew she kept what cash she had in the narrow, middle dresser drawer. He jerked it open. There, folded in the back corner of the drawer amidst hair pins and a few pieces of cheap costume jewelry, was a ten-dollar bill. That was all. He grabbed it and stuffed it into the pocket with the knife. Grabbing the backpack, he dashed out the front door and into the woods. He did not look back at the open door that he had slammed against the aluminum side of the trailer. The rod and reel had fallen unnoticed to the ground. Nor did he look back down toward the river. There was no need to. He knew what was there.

He ran along the dark path until he felt his lungs would explode. He stumbled on an exposed root, scraping his hands and arms. His left elbow was scraped the worse and blood trailed down his forearm. When he got to the creek he threw the backpack aside and knelt down, breathless, splashing the cool water onto his face and neck, then the scraped elbow. His throat and mouth were dry and burned with thirst, but he knew better than to drink the creek water.

He finally caught his breath and looked back over his shoulder down the path. The woods were silent as light. Nothing moved. He stood up and took another deep breath. Then he grabbed the backpack and leaped over the narrow creek. He began to run again, but slower, a steady jog. His calf muscles ached and there did not seem to be enough air to breathe in the deep woods.

After a while he slowed to his pace to a walk, but it was a fast one. Although he was conscious only of his own breathing and the hushed fall of his footsteps, he kept glancing back over his shoulder at the path behind him. All I need to do is make it to the county road, he kept telling himself. I can catch a ride there. To where he didn't know or care. It didn't matter. Surely they couldn't catch him now.

Ahead of him the path curved and disappeared into the blackness of the forest. The canopy of trees was thick overhead and blocked out most of the sunlight, but not the heat and humidity. Then he heard the muted sound of an automobile passing up ahead in the distance. I am close the highway, he thought, and his paced quickened. As he rounded the turn of the path, he saw sunlight up beyond him in an opening in the trees. It was the highway.

A deep ditch ran along the edge of the trees beyond which was the narrow shoulder of the road. The road was not a busy one, but he had seen several cars speed by as he approached it from the forest path. He half slid down the steep bank of the ditch and scrambled up the other side.

Standing on the shoulder, he dropped the backpack and brushed off the red clay dust with his hands. He wasn't that far from Russellville now and he should be able to hitch a ride. He began to walk on the edge of the pavement. There were no houses along this section of the road and the forest pressed it on both sides as far ahead as he could see. The sky had become overcast, but there was still a hot thickness to the air. Comin' up a cloud, he thought, it'll be rainin' by evening.

A few vehicles sped past him, mostly pickup trucks. There were a couple of cars with Florida tags. Tourist headed for the mountains. The old people inside had looked at him curiously as the drivers veered unnecessarily toward the center of the road as if to avoid hitting him. With each approaching car, he turned and walked backward facing it, his thumb extended from his thin right hand. A couple of them had honked their horns and waved, but none stopped. He walked on.

He stayed walking along the road, trying now not to think too much. Just get away. But he couldn't make sense of it, what he had seen back at the trailer. It had to be by chance, he thought, that the two drifters had come to the trailer. The same ones who had harassed him at Sadler's Creek. They were just roaming around. What had they done to his aunt, and why? Just bad men, he reckoned. But they had not seen him when he came down the path after getting off the school bus. He knew that much. So, he reasoned, there's no connection to me that they know of. Maybe I'm safe, but I can't take a chance. I got to run. The only place he knew to run to was Troy, over in Wofford county. Maybe his father was out of jail. Maybe he could find him. He convinced himself that he could. He had to.

No cars passed by for a while. The forest crowding the road on either side was dark and silent. He heard only the sound of his own breathing. Then he heard something, a vehicle, and glanced back to see it approaching. He stopped and turned to face it, his thumb pointing down the road. The faded, red Cadillac convertible, its top down, slowed and passed him before pulling partly onto the shoulder ahead. Attached to the rear bumper was a small, silver travel trailer. The driver, a man, had not seemed to see the boy as he passed by. But he had. As the car came to a stop, the Boy jogged to it.

"Need a ride, son?" came the inane, but inevitable question.

"I reckon I do."

"Where you headed?"

"Down this road here. Might be going over to Troy."

"Well, I ain't going near that far. Just the other side of Russellville."

"That's good. Don't matter," the Boy replied. He opened the door and climbed in. He held the book bag in his lap.

"You can throw that in the back seat if you want to," said the driver.

"Nah, I'll just hold it. We ain't going far you said." He looked straight ahead at the road and did not look over at the driver as he pulled back onto the road. The Cadillac gained speed rapidly despite the tug of the trailer.

"Headed over to Troy, eh?" the driver asked, his voice loud and resonant over the noise of the convertible's rushing air and the deep, mellow rumble of the V-8 engine.

"Might be," the Boy replied flatly, staring ahead.

"You live in Troy?"

"No."

"Some of your people over there, I suppose?"

"Just my daddy."

"Going to see you father, huh?"

"Yeah, I guess I am."

"He know you coming?"

"No."

They drove in silence, then the man looked at him.

"Well, tell me son, you been saved?"

Yeah, saved by you from getting myself killed, the Boy thought, but he knew that wasn't what the driver meant.

"I guess so. I don't really know."

"You got to know! Ain't you been baptized, old as you look to be?"

"No."

"You need to be," said the driver.

"Why?"

"Why, son? To save your soul from eternal damnation! From hell fire itself! That's why!"

"I never been to church much."

"Well, today's your day of reckoning I'd say. I'm a preacher. I mean I'm a real preacher."

"A preacher?"

"That's right, a preacher. An evangelist to be more exact. Do you know what an evangelist is?"

"No, not really. Maybe like them on television always wanting to swap you something for your money?

"No, they're wolves in sheep's clothing. They're after your money all right, most of 'em. And women too, some of 'em. I'm after lost souls. I'm the real deal. Called by the Lord Hisself. Might say I'm a prophet, too. I'll baptize you tonight if you be willing and confess your sins."

Finally, the Boy looked over at the driver—the preacher. He was red-faced with a prominent aquiline nose. What he could see of his eyes they were pools of dark, but lively intensity. His hair was thick and unnaturally black and swept back from his forehead. The thin lips curled down slightly, giving him not quite a sinister look, but you weren't sure you could trust him either. He wore a brightly colored polyester Hawaiian shirt. Don't look much like a preacher, thought the Boy. Just kind of weird.

"I'll be on down the road way past Russellville by dark. Won't be no time for baptizin'."

"We'll see about that, I reckon, young fella. There's rain in the air. You don't want to be out here hitchhiking in the rain, now do you?"

"Rain don't bother me none. I've been wet before."

When he said this, the image of his aunt's corpulent body being rolled over into the river by the two men flashed before him. They might be waiting for him to come home or they might be driving around looking for him. But he hadn't seen a car parked on the road near the trailer. If they looked around the trailer they would know someone else lived there besides his aunt. He had left the proofs of his school pictures on the chest of drawers. They might see them. He had meant to take them back to school that morning, but had forgotten about them; he had no money for school pictures. They'd seen him that day up on Sadler's Creek. They'd gotten a good look for sure. Even as the warm air flowed over him, a sudden, quick shiver passed through his body.

The convertible slowed as it passed the town-limit sign. There wasn't much to Russellville, less a town than a village, if that. They drove past the hardware store, then a café with a large plate glassed window almost opaque with condensation and encrusted street dust. There was a crumbling, boarded-up, two-story red-brick building. It once had been a sanitarium according to the faded and peeling black letters on the door. Across from the service station the car stopped at the town's one traffic light as it turned red. Two barefoot children held the hands of an old woman crossing the street in front of them headed for the small, sad grocery store on the other side.

"Reckon I'll get out here. Thanks for the ride, preacher," he said, reaching down for the chrome door handle.

"Just sit tight, son. I'm setting up just a mile or so the other side of town, straight ahead. It'll get you a little closer to where you're going."

"All right." He released the handle and leaned forward in the seat, his arms folded across the backpack in his lap. He continued to look straight ahead and not at the preacher.

The preacher smiled slightly, as if to himself. The light changed and the Cadillac slowly accelerated. Two more blocks and Russellville was in the rearview mirror.

Up ahead, on the right, the Boy saw a large sign made out of a sheet of weathered, dingy painted, plywood. On it, in neatly hand-printed letters of red were the words, TENT MEETING REVIVIAL TONIGHT. And beneath this, written in smaller letters, GOSPEL PREACHING + HEALING, and below this, REPENT, NEIGHBOR, OR BURN IN HELL. Red flames had been crudely painted in each corner of the sign. The car slowed and pulled off the road onto the vacant lot beside the sign.

"Well, this is it, son. This is where I'll be preaching and saving souls for the next week or so, or however long the Lord leads me to stay here. The call is mighty strong so I reckon they's lots of sinners in these parts."

"That you?" asked the Boy, nodding toward the sign.

"Yessiree, Bob! I reckon it is. I'm well known in some parts."

"Well, *I* never heard of you."

"Don't matter. I ain't from around here. But I'm here now."

The lot, more of a large open field, was treeless and thickly carpeted with weeds—mostly brome, milkweed, and dandelions. It was dry and dusty. In the distance was what looked to be a long-ago plowed patch of depleted soil now covered in crab grass and beyond that, a line of pine trees. On the ground, just beyond the car, was a huge stack of neatly folded canvas, a pile of wooden posts, and steel spikes. There were coils of thick, hemp rope on top of the canvas. Also, there was a large galvanized trough-like tub on the ground beside these items.

"It don't look like much right now," the preacher offered, "but soon as I get the tent put up and the light poles a-working it's a wonder to behold. Especially at night. Praise the Lord!"

The Boy said nothing, but got out of the car and held the backpack by one strap over his shoulder. The preacher grinned and reached behind the front seat and pulled a plastic bottle of water from a beat-up Coleman cooler sitting on the floor board.

"Here," he said, and tossed the bottle of water to the Boy who was not looking at him. The bottle bounced off the car door and landed in the dust at the Boy's feet.

"Sorry, I thought you were looking. I expect you must be thirsty from the looks of you. Meant to offer you the water back there at the red light."

"Thanks," said the Boy. He dropped the backpack and picked up the bottle. It was cold from the cooler and caked with the dust from the ground. But he was past thirsty. He unscrewed the cap and gulped down half of the ice-cold liquid.

"Say, you were a mite dry."

The Boy wiped the dirt from the bottle as best he could and placed it in the backpack. He then hoisted it onto this back and, adjusting the straps on his thin shoulders, walked back toward the highway. There was a dull roar of thunder in the distance. He turned back toward the preacher who had opened the trunk of the Cadillac, now partially obscured by the travel trailer.

"Thanks for the water, Preacher," he said and walked away toward the highway glancing up at the darkening western clouds.

The preacher hurried toward him in long, purposeful strides.

"Oh, now wait a minute, boy. What's the hurry? Stay awhile and help me set up my trailer. I'll cook us some supper. You bound to be hungry. I bet as hungry as you were thirsty." The preacher was bound to baptize him, and he knew it.

"Nah, I got to hitch a ride. It's fixin' to come up a cloud. I heard thunder."

"I heard it, too," said the preacher. "It might very well be the voice of the Lord Hisself. We got to listen for the Lord. Don't you know that, boy?

"I didn't hear the Lord; I heard thunder." A pickup sped by on the highway. "That might have been my ride," he said impatiently. He started to walk away, but the preacher placed a hand on his shoulder. The Boy pulled away. He did not like the strange feel of the preacher's claw-like grip. The face of Mr. Galloway flashed across his mind for an instant.

"It's going to be dark soon and pouring cats and dogs out here. Likely all night," the preacher said, his voice changing, taking on a more soothing conciliatory tone. "That trailer's going to be nice and cozy on a night like we got coming. Nice soft, clean bed. I got some venison stew a feller over in north Georgia gave me. Gave it to me after I saved him."

The Boy looked away. He was tired and hungry. Those two men were likely out looking for him. They might even see him hitchhiking. The heavy air had begun to feel damp. It looked to be a storm, a hard rain.

"You just tryin' to get me where you can baptize me, ain't you? I believe that's what you thinkin' about."

"Oh, I won't deny it, boy. Never would. I purely and surely wish for you to give your soul to the Lord and go to Glory when you die, whenever that might be. We don't know. Could be soon, you know, or a while longer. But I won't try to force you to get saved. Don't work like that anyhow. I reckon I just want some company. You know what I mean?"

"No."

There was a long silence between them. The Boy, his lips tightly pursed, was thinking, weighing his options.

"Much to getting that trailer set up?" he finally asked.

"Naw, ain't nothing to it. I'll just pull it up a ways onto that clear, level spot over there. Then just jack it up to level it some more. That's all. Not much to it," the preacher said. There was almost an excitement in his voice.

"All right," said the Boy.

"That's good. Real good."

"But I'm leaving at first light, rain or shine."

"I reckon you will, boy, I reckon you will."

The Preacher pulled the small trailer up onto the level spot and disconnected it from the car. The Boy followed him and stood watching. The Preacher worked the jacks at each corner of the camper. He would occasionally step back and eye his work, but finally announced that the trailer was adequately level for habitation.

"What about the tent? Ain't you going to put it up before it starts raining?"

"Oh, naw," laughed the Preacher. "That's a big job. Takes a crew. I hired me some colored fellas I came upon a ways back. Saw them sitting on the porch. Stopped and talked and gave them my witness. Looked like they needed the work, which they said they did, so they coming in here in the morning to put the tent up. Bright and early."

"But your sign says there's a tent meeting revival tonight."

"It always says that. It'll read true in the morning. Folks ain't going come out in the rain to a tent meeting anyhow. They just ain't thirsty enough to want to drink from the fountain of the Word, I reckon. Anyway, come on in and see my humble abode. I think you'll like it. You ever been inside a trailer before, sonny?"

The Boy almost laughed out loud at the irony.

"Yeah, I been in a trailer before." Reckon, he thought, that's pretty much all I ever lived in. Well, almost ever.

"Not a travel-trailer like my camper here, I'll bet."

"No."

"My home away from home I call it," said the Preacher.

"You got a house somewhere?" asked the Boy.

"Home is where the heart is, ain't it?"

"I don't know," answered the Boy. "I never had a home, not a real one anyway." And, he thought, I ain't sure if I even have a heart anymore.

Huge drops of rain began to fall, splattering in the dust around them. The Boy glanced up at the dark, roiling sky and then back out at the road. The Preacher stepped up onto the narrow metal steps welded to the trailer's frame and opened the door. He stood in the doorway, looking down at the Boy.

"You better get on in here before you get wet or lightning struck." He moved back from the door and the Boy followed him into the tiny shelter.

CHAPTER 9

The police car, coated in red dust, turned onto River Road. The Deputy drove slowly as he scanned the shoulder, and up ahead for houses and other signs of human habitation in the sad and scrubby landscape to either side. He finally spotted a mailbox near the left side of the road and eased the car up to it. Reading the name scrawled there, he parked the car. The path beside the mailbox sloped down sharply through a field of weeds and gullies, and ended in the dirt yard of a small unpainted house.

He took the path, but stumbled as he stepped off the tar and gravel payment, steadying himself by grabbing onto the mailbox which itself leaned precariously toward the road. Nothing here seemed to be straight. Nothing erect or linear. The land slanted, what trees remained were gnarled and crooked, the small house below seemed to be canted at all angles, and the landscape itself shimmered in the heat giving it a sense of slow waves in motion.

As he approached the shack, the large dark dog slid from under the low porch, its growl low and hoarse in its throat, teeth bared.

"Whoa now, boy," said the Deputy calmly, holding up both palms, arms extended. "Take it easy now."

But the dog did not back down nor did it appear any less menacing to the intruder. Just as the Deputy started to call out to the sagging, insentient house, a man in overalls and shirtless appeared from around back. Like everything else here there was nothing vertical about him. His thin shoulders were hunched over and he bent slightly forward at the waist. Bad back, thought the Deputy. Even in the baggy overalls the bow of his legs was apparent. He looked hard at the Deputy and then glanced at the police car parked up on the road. He spat a black stream which splattered on the dusty ground and was quickly absorbed by it.

"Hush, Butch. You git back under the house. Go on now, I mean it. Go on, boy, 'fore I kick the shit out you." The dog's tail relaxed and with ears back, reluctantly slunk back under the porch steps.

"Mean dog," said the Deputy from across the yard.

"That's what I got him fer. You can come on in the yard if you want."

The policeman stepped over a patch of low growing briars onto the dirt expanse of the yard.

"Don't hurt to have a good guard dog, I don't reckon."

"Something I can do fer you?" asked the old man shoving both hands into his pockets, the fingers of one lightly touching the revolver.

"Mail box up there says 'Redden'."

"That's right."

"You Redden?"

"I reckon I am."

"I'm looking for a kid. A boy. Thirteen, fourteen maybe. Thought he might be some kin."

"What's he done?" asked the old man.

"Nothing as I know of."

"Why you lookin' for him then?"

"Just need to talk to him, that's all. Police business."

"Trouble's what you mean. Well, I can't help you none. He ain't no Redden, I can tell you that much."

"Don't matter. It was a long shot anyhow. Sorry to bother you." said the Deputy, removing his hat and wiping his forehead with a handkerchief. He then wiped the sweatband of the hat and placed it back on his head. He turned to leave, stepping back over the briars on the path.

"Why's this young'un so popler, anyway?" the old man said to his back.

"What do you mean—popular?" asked the Deputy, turning toward him.

"I don't reckon you the only one lookin' for the kid."

"You know of somebody else trying to find a boy, one like I described?"

"I reckon I do. Two ole boys come by here a day or two ago, I don't recollect exactly. Askin' about a young'un just like you doin' now. Car broke down up on the highway they said. Said they got kin around here. Mentioned the young'un, same as you.

"Is that right?" said the Deputy, stepping back into the yard.

"They was a scroungy pair. Up to no good, fer as I could tell. They was lyin'. I knew it and I run 'em off."

"What did they look like? Did you get a good look at them?"

'Course I did. They was standin' close as you and me. One was a big ole feller, not fat, just big. The other was scrawny as hell. Neither one of 'em looked like they'd a bath in a month. I figured they was trouble so I got rid of 'em. Run 'em off. They was scared of old Butch yonder."

"So they just wandered off?" asked the Deputy.

"More or less. They's a boy what's been stayin' down the road there a piece." The old man motioned slightly with his head, toward the end of River Road where it disappeared into a clump of trees. "But I don't know 'em. Ole gal moved in the trailer a while back. Keeps to herself fer as I know. I seen the boy fishing on the river bank a couple of times"

"Why didn't you tell me all this in the first place?"

"Well, I tellin' you now, ain't I? Besides, I don't want to get mixed up in no trouble. I keep to myself and expect neighbors to do the same. Don't want no trouble. Not if I can help it."

"All right. I'm much obliged for the information anyhow. Did you ever speak to the boy? I mean talk to him when you saw him fishing."

"Naw, I was up the river a ways shootin' squirrels. I could just see him down on the bank fishing. That's all. Not close up. I didn't have nothin' to say to him. He's mindin' his own business like I was mindin' mine. No cause to speak."

"Okay," said the Deputy. "You say that trailer's down this road apiece? How far?"

"Yeah, half a mile or so. The road runs out down there. Old blue trailer, all dented and beat up like a tin can."

The Deputy trudged back up the long hill to his car. He started the engine and eased the patrol car on down River Road.

He easily spotted the house trailer from the road and it looked pretty much as the old man said. It stood down off the road much like the old man's cabin, but the sloping field was much more eroded and slashed with deep, red gullies. There were thick woods to the left of the trailer and the wide muddy river ran behind it, down another steep slope. He parked the car and started down.

As the ground leveled out near the trailer he could see the front door standing partially open. He glanced around the bare, dirt yard and spotted the scattered cigarette butts and empty beer cans over near the plank bench. In the heat nothing moved and a pall of silence hung heavily in the air, pressing against him. He then negotiated the steps—several of the cinder blocks were missing— and tapped several times on the door. He listened. Nothing. He pushed open the door and entered the living room. It was in total disarray, furniture overturned, lamps without electrical cords, a mirror shattered. In the kitchen he found much the same. Dishes broken and the door to the nearly empty refrigerator stood open. In this closed space the air was heavy and fetid with the stench of rotting scraps of food and of urine.

He made his way through the trailer and finally to what was the Boy's room. A pile of textbooks was heaped on the floor beside the bed. He picked one up, a math book. Seventh or eighth grade, he almost said aloud. The Boy's. Something had happened here. Something not good. The two strangers, the men, might well be the same ones who had come by the store the woman had told him about. They had found the Boy, maybe. He had known them or seen them. There was a connection. There had to be. He had picked up the scent, but it was probably too late to help the woman. Where was she? Yes, for sure, something bad happened here.

He walked down the steep hill behind the trailer to the river. The low bank was littered with scraps of paper, food wrappers, and empty cans. The bank itself was bare dank earth, black, almost mud. At a spot near the edge of the water he noticed shoe prints, mostly slick smears in the soft earth. But they looked fresh. Strangely, but perhaps not so strange, a brown electrical cord lay on the ground near the scuffed ground. He crouched down, his weight on his toes of his shoes, and examined the cord. From a lamp or appliance, he thought. He looked out across the sluggardly moving river which seemed reluctant to move at all. Something bad happened here.

The Deputy trudged back up the hill and stood outside the trailer. He'd need to report what he'd found here, and he would—soon. But his mind was on the Boy. And the killer—or killers. If the Boy was in the river they'd find him. His body. Hers too if she was there. The pile of books in the bedroom didn't add up though. Was there a chance that he had gotten away? Inexplicably, he felt that the Boy was still alive, or could be. But where? If he was alive he was probably scared and on the run, or hiding out someplace. The Deputy considered going into the woods beyond the trailer. Maybe he was there. But he knew that would be a real long shot now. Actually, he didn't know what to do. The Boy would turn up someplace if he was still alive. A kid like that had to. He'd just have to wait and see. He'd already spent too much time in McBee County. He needed to get back.

He did not go back into the trailer. There was no need too. He made his way back up the steep hill to his car and drove away. Back to Troy.

"This ain't too bad now is it, boy?"

"It's all right."

With approaching darkness, the rain had moved in fast and hard. It had at first beat a slow, staccato rhythm on the metal roof of the trailer, but was soon a resounding low, constant roar.

"A little warm though. You can reach there behind you and roll out that window some."

The Boy turned the plastic crank, opening the window. The wet air was warm, but offered a little relief. He wiped his forehead with the sleeve of his tee shirt. A sudden, sharp crack of thunder startled him briefly. He was glad that he was not out in the rain, but he would not let the Preacher know this. Anyway, in the morning he'd be gone.

The trailer was small and cramped and there was no bed to be seen. Probably folded out from the wall or something, he thought. In the front corner was a tiny galley kitchen, just enough room for a person to stand. This is where the Preacher stood now, his arms folded across his chest looking at him.

"You just sit down there on the sofa. I'll get this here stew cooking."

He sat down on what the Preacher called a sofa—just a narrow, padded bench seat, yellow and stained. He leaned against the wall and stared into the wet darkness through the window across from him.

"Now look here," said the Preacher as he moved into the small space in front of the Boy. He reached over and behind him. "Just stand over there for a minute while I make us a table." The Boy stood up and moved away as far as he could. The wall behind where he had been sitting was actually a hinged table top which the preacher lowered. "This here's the table. We can eat off it, you know. It's my bed too. I mean, under this sofa here is a foam mattress, so it works out pretty good. You can sit back down. Stew's about ready. Smell's good, don't it." The Preacher shuffled back into the galley.

He wondered where he would sleep. With the table—or bed—folded down there wasn't room in the camper for another bed. Maybe on the floor beneath the Preacher, he didn't know. It didn't really matter to him as long as he could be out of here in the morning.

The Preacher spread a newspaper on the table. "Don't have quite *all* the comforts of home here, but this'll do for a tablecloth, I guess." He then returned to the kitchen.

The Boy looked down at the newspaper. It was not today's or yesterday's. Then he saw it. UNIDENTFIED WOMAN FOUND STABBED NEAR SADLER'S CREEK. His heart stopped. He began to read. The description of the dead woman. It was her. It had to be; he knew it. She was last seen with two men. The two men. Sketchy descriptions, but them just the same. He knew it.

"You pale as a ghost," said the Preacher as he set two bowls of stew on the table. "You feeling okay?"

"Yeah, I'm all right," answered the Boy. "I'm all right," he repeated as he absentmindedly ate the stew, staring down into the bowl of food before him.

The Preacher didn't say anything else while they ate. He finally dropped the spoon into his empty bowl and pushed himself away from the table. He eyed the Boy.

"Reckon I was right about the rain. Don't seem like it's anywhere near letting up." The Boy didn't look at him.

"But then again, doesn't matter now does it? We're high and dry in here. You'd a been a drowned rat if you'd stayed on the road. That's for sure." The Boy didn't respond. "It's mighty nice to have company, I can tell you that much."

"Where am I supposed to sleep?" the Boy finally asked.

"Oh, I got a place for you, that's for sure," said the Preacher. "Nice and cozy, too."

"I don't see a place."

The Preacher pointed toward the rear of the trailer, opposite the galley kitchen. The Boy turned to see where he was pointing.

"It's up there," said the preacher. There was a shelf at the rear, about two feet from the low ceiling, that ran across the width of the trailer, a kind of a bunk. "I'll just get you a blanket when you're ready to go to sleep. You can just climb up there and snooze away."

The Boy stared up at the shelf— the bunk. The rain was relentless and he suddenly realized how tired he was. And he was, for the moment at least, safe.

"I'm ready to go to sleep now."

"Sure thing," said the preacher. He stood up and started to clear away the table. "I reckon we both got big days ahead of us tomorrow. And you been traveling from— from where did you say?" The Boy looked out into the darkness as if he hadn't heard him. "Well, I guess it doesn't matter, now does it? Anyway, you're headed for Troy in the morning and I got to get things ready for the meeting tomorrow night. I just hope this storm has come through by then."

"It won't matter. I told you I was leaving in the morning."

"Now don't go getting all riled up. I know what you said and I expect you'll be gone first light. Just hope it ain't raining. That's all I meant."

The Preacher raised the seat of the small sofa and pulled out an army-surplus blanket. The Boy took the blanket and pulled himself up onto the bunk. The Preacher then placed a thick piece of foam rubber on his bed, what had been the table. The Boy lay there, his head resting on the backpack, watching him make his bed and then puttering around the kitchen. Finally, he seemed to run out of things to do and reached for the light switch.

"Well, that's about it. I hope you sleep good," said the Preacher as he flicked off the light. The Boy could hear him fumbling below with his trousers. He then turned on his back as he felt the ceiling to be pressing down upon him, but not in a bad way. The rain continued to beat down on the trailer. Just inches from my face, he thought. He felt alone and he knew that he was, but for now it was all right. He had survived the day.

But what about the dead woman and the two men. They'd killed his aunt. It had to be them. Somehow found where I lived. But how? He hadn't spoken to anyone about meeting them on the creek. But somehow they had found him, or at least his aunt. It just didn't add up, but he was scared. They were after him. He could feel it. But he'd be gone in the morning. First thing.

"Thanks for the stew," the Boy finally said in the darkness, but the Preacher only answered with a soft snore. He lay there in the darkness, feeling an in explicable comfort from the rain outside and the warmth of the trailer. It was good for now, he thought, but not for tomorrow. Not unless I can find my daddy. He then fell into a deep, dreamless sleep. The sleep of a boy.

"Get up! You got to get up now!" He turned in the bunk to find the preacher in his face. He was gripping the edge with both hands, shaking it. The rain had stopped. It was not yet fully light and the Preacher's face was like a gray mirage in the predawn. Or was it a dream?

"What?" the Boy mumbled, half asleep.

"Look, sonny, I've got to get out of here, and fast. Sun'll be up soon. I'll help you get your things together."

The Boy swung his legs over the side of the bunk, but still had to hold his head down from the low ceiling. "I ain't got no things. Just my backpack."

"Well, get it and get out to the road. You might get a ride this early."

The Boy pushed himself off the edge of the bunk and onto the floor. The table—the bed— was gone. Folded and latched against the wall. The backpack was in the floor beside the door.

"Look, I hate to run you off like this, but something's come up. I mean, I got to be leaving here! I mean now! You said yourself you wanted to be gone at the crack of dawn anyway." The Preacher was animated and nervous.

"I know what I said. I'm glad to be up and out of here. But what about your tent revival and all the people you were goin' to save?"

"Plans change and you got to—uh—be ready to change with them. You know how it is," the Preacher said impatiently.

Yeah, he thought, I know how it is. Plans change.

"All right," said the Boy, picking up his backpack. "I'm goin'."

"Look here, sonny, it's just, well, to tell you the truth I got into a little trouble down in a place called Langley—over in Georgia—a while back. After a meeting one night I was counseling, consoling really, one of the flock. Young girl actually. Her mama walked in on us—I mean I was just praying with her and, like I said, consoling the child. But her mama didn't see it that way. I just don't know about people interfering with God's work. Satan's handiwork, I reckon, them actin' like that. But anyway, I skedaddled fast as I could, but they're on my tail now! Got a message a little while ago. A text on my phone."

He pushed open the door and stepped out into the still, wet coolness of the early morning. He noticed that the trailer was already hooked to the rear of the Cadillac. He looked up at the Preacher still standing in the doorway, and then turned and walked toward the road.

"I sure wish I coulda baptized you, sonny. I purely and surely do,"
the Preacher called to his back.

By the time he reached the road, the preacher had pulled out, and with trailer in tow, sped away. He stood by the road for a moment and watched as the taillights faded in the waning darkness. The he turned and began to walk along the deserted road.

CHAPTER 11

The large room was barracks-like, with its high ceiling and four rows of iron-framed cots that ran parallel to the length of it. The floor, like the walls, was concrete and both had been leveled over time with many coats of light-gray oil-paint. Huge industrial-like lights with broad round metal shades were mounted close to the ceiling, covering the room with harsh, garish light that afforded no shadows. There were no windows, not as such, but at intervals narrow vertical slits were cut into the wall, up high, out of reach and useless, almost to the ceiling. The length of each slit was bisected by a single steel bar. Little light or air from the outside passed through the slits. The room was always stifling hot, never comfortable. In the winter, a huge fan blasted hot air from a low, rumbling oil-fired boiler through a large duct terminal at one end of the room. It seemed to never stop, day or night, and ran well into springtime. As summer approached, the boiler was shut down and the room became an airless oven in the Southern heat. Except for the most inclement weather, the sixty men who slept in the room much preferred to be outdoors. Being in a county prison camp, they were usually accommodated. Although they were wards of the county and officially housed in a Department of Corrections facility, they were in the South, where they were still referred to euphemistically as being on *the chain-gang*.

It was near lights-out and final count. Two of the men sat on the edge of their cots, in thread-bare cotton undershorts, facing each other, their exposed skin glistening in the hot brightness. They spoke, their voices low.

"What's it feel like, Posey? Gettin' out, I mean."

"It don't feel like nothing."

"The hell it don't! This is my third stretch and it always felt mighty good walkin' out of here a free man."

"How come you back in here so soon, then?"

"You know how it is on the outside. My mama says I run with the wrong crowd."

"Hell, Snake, you *are* the wrong crowd," Posey said without expression.

"Yeah, well, I might be at that, but I'd sure be happy if I was gettin' out of here tomorrow. Happier than you appear to be. You a strange dude, Posey."

"Nothing strange about me."

"Well, maybe strange ain't the right word," said Snake.

"Maybe it ain't."

"Whatcha goin' do?'

"About what?

"You know, once you're out of here."

"I don't know. Get as far away from Wofford County as I can, for sure," answered Posey.

"You got folks pickin' you up in the mornin', I reckon."

Posey didn't answer, but turned and stretched out on his cot, staring at the ceiling, his hands locked behind his head. He knew there would be no one waiting for him in the morning when he stepped into the light of freedom. Those bridges had long since been burned and he didn't plan on building any new ones.

"Naw, nobody. Nobody as I know of," said Posey, still gazing at the ceiling.

"You can get into Troy easy enough from here. You got a place to stay?" asked Snake.

"No, but I sure ain't going to Troy except maybe to catch a bus."

"I reckon you got some jack," Snake said, but it was more a question than a statement of fact.

"Not much. I figured they'd give a little to live on, seein' I been in here so long."

"They who?" Snake asked, truly puzzled.

"They. The county. I been a ward of this sorry-ass county for near five years."

Snake chuckled. "The county ain't going to give you shit! You walk out them iron doors tomorrow and you on your own. I can promise you that much. *The county.* I swear!"

"Shut up."

"I'm just tellin' you like it is, that's all. I been around the block a few times. I know how it works, and how it don't work." The two men were silent for a few moments, Posey lying there staring at the ceiling, Snake sitting on the edge of his cot, staring at the floor, perspiration dripping off the tip of his nose and puddling on the floor between his feet. Finally, Snake continued. "You ever work? Know how to do anything? I mean anything useful and close to legal."

After a brief pause, Posey spoke. "I can hang gutters. I worked with sheet metal some. That's about it."

"Shit, man, you got it made then. You just need to get over around Corinth. They buildin' stuff over there like they ain't no tomorrow. You could be hired on before sundown tomorrow."

"Maybe, but I sure as hell ain't going near Corinth neither. I figure I might head up toward Nashville."

"Nashville? How come Nashville?" asked Snake.

"Mainly 'cause I ain't never been there. It's a pretty big town and nobody'll know me there. That's the way I like things."

"Start off clean, you mean?"

"No," said Posey, "that ain't what I mean."

Just then a hoarse but loud voice boomed from the far end of the long room, near the steel-doored entrance.

"All right, ladies. Hit them bunks. Gonna count y'all's sorry asses and turn off the lights."

The uniformed guard cinched up his trousers over a protruding belly and pushed the visor cap back on his forehead. He walked slowly down the aisle between the cots. As he passed each one, he tapped the iron frame lightly with a nightstick and counted the man lying on it. He tapped Snakes's cot frame, counted him, and move to the next cot.

"Well, well, Posey. Looks like you finally getting out of here. Kind of hate to see you go, if you know what I mean. We don't get many like you anymore. You remind me of the old days. Almost brings a tear to my eye."

Posey didn't respond to the guard's sarcasm, but remained motionless and silent, still staring at the ceiling. He may not have even heard him.

The fat guard smirked and moved on to finish his tapping and counting. He then strode back to the far end where the door was, and switched off the glaring overhead lights. The room was at once bathed in darkness and hot, stale air, with nothing but the smell of men and the sounds of them breathing in their misery. The steel door slammed shut and sent a dull echo down the length of the room. Then all heard the familiar and hated sound of the tumblers of the heavy, steel lock fall into place.

Posey sat alone on his cot. He was fully dressed in the blue faded denim uniform of a prisoner. The only throwback to the black and white striped chain gang uniform of a long-past era was the white stripe that ran down the outside of each pant leg. It was subtle, but it was there. He heard the steel door at the far end bang open. And then the sharp tap of shoes on the concrete floor. He finally looked up as a guard approached.

"Come on, Posey. Gotta get you over to the office so we can process you outta here. Come on."

Posey stood up. The guard continued. "Turn around. We walking across the yard. I got to put these cuffs on you."

"Damn, Bannister, I'm getting out of this shit hole in a few minutes. I don't see no call for handcuffs."

"Don't go starting to give me a hard time, Posey. You know the rules. It's all standard procedure. Come on, let's get on with it. It's near noon and I don't want to be late for dinner. Wife packed me fried chicken and potato salad."

Posey looked at the guard briefly then turned away from him as the cuffs clicked locked against his wrist. They left the building and walked across a wide expanse of asphalt yard toward the prison offices. Once inside, the guard guided Posey to a straight chair at a bare metal table and removed the cuffs. Another uniformed officer entered the room.

"He's all yours, chief," said the guard. "I'm going to dinner."

The officer did not acknowledge Bannister as he exited, but placed a large brown paper bag on the table and sat down.

"Here's your things, Posey. Just what they brought you in here with, nothing more, nothing less." Posey looked at the paper bag but did not respond. "I reckon I got to count it out to you. Wouldn't want you accusing the county of keeping something that belonged to one of our illustrious inmates, now would we?" The officer turned the bag up and spread its few contents on the table. "That look about right to you?"

"I reckon," Posey said, almost in a mumble.

"Let's see now, a pair of blue jeans not in the best of repair, a green cotton tee shirt, a denim jacket, a pair of Nikes that's seen better days, and two socks. This here's your billfold." The officer spread open the wallet for Posey to examine. "Three one-dollar bills. That's it, Posey. Ain't much, is it?"

Posey did not respond.

"You can change clothes in here, since you showered this morning. You can keep the underwear you got on, seeing you didn't wear any in. Socks too. They're in a mite better shape that these on the table."

The prisoner stood up and removed the prison uniform and donned the clothes heaped on the table. The officer sat down at the table and scribbled on some forms. Posey stood beside the chair. The officer finally looked up at him.

"Damn if you ain't a sight, Posey. Pick up those prison clothes off the floor and fold them and put them on the table. Fold them right, too."

Posey bent over and picked the clothes up and folded them neatly, then placed them in the middle of the table.

"Sit back down. We got some papers to fill out. Damn if you convicts ain't more trouble getting out than you are getting in."

For the next thirty minutes the officer slowly and painfully went through the various forms before him. Each question or statement he read aloud, mostly to himself. Occasionally, there was information he required from Posey, but his answers were short and scant. Finally, the officer pushed a form across the table to Posey.

"Sign down there at the bottom where I drew an 'x'." It was signed and slid back to the officer, who examined the completed form and put it in a stack with the others. He then looked hard at the soon-to-be free man across from him.

"Damn, Posey, you ain't accomplished much in nearly five years here."

"Ain't much to accomplish locked up in this hell-hole."

"That true enough, but some men do. Not men like you though. I'll give you one thing. You managed not to get transferred to the state pen in Columbia. With all the trouble you caused here, I figured the warden would have shipped your ass off a long time ago."

"Guess he likes me," Posey said, not smiling.

"Most men come in, do their two or three years and go on their way. At least until next time. Took you nearly five. You a hard case ain't you, Posey."

"Just some bad luck, I reckon."

The officer shook his head and then straightened the stack of forms. Posey finally moved, squirming impatiently in his chair. The officer then stood up.

"Well, that's about it. You got a girlfriend or some of your hoodlum buddies picking you up outside."

"No."

"You're trouble, Posey. I expect I'll see you again before too long." Posey was silent. "You got family don't you, around here or over in McBee County? File shows you got a young'un someplace. A boy, I believe."

"Yeah, I got a kid. I don't know where he is."

"Don't sound much like you care where he is. He grown?"

"He'd be about thirteen now, I'd reckon. Maybe fourteen. Anyway, ain't nothing I could do for him."

"What about his mama. He with her?"

"She's dead, been dead. Anyway, I ain't here to tell you my life story. I'm ready to get the hell out of here."

"You a hard case, Posey," the officer repeated, and then slipped a piece of paper from a small envelop and slid it across to Posey.

"What's this?"

"It's a chit for a meal. You won't be eating dinner here. It's good about any place around here. County guarantees payment."

"A chit for my dinner!" said Posey angrily. "I got three dollars to my name. County's got to give me some money to get started on. I ain't even got a place to sleep tonight! Surely I got some back pay for all the road work we done."

"You spent it all on cigarettes, Posey, and likely contraband too."

"I figured on getting something from y'all here when I got out."

"Sorry, Posey, that ain't the way it works. You people all alike. Act any way you want to and then think the county or state or somebody owes you something. Just feeding from the trough. Anyway, you're done here. This door behind me leads out to the hallway. Down that hallway is the entrance—exit in your case—to this place. See you around, Posey, but I hope it ain't here again."

"You won't see none of me around these parts. I can guarantee that." Posey stood and picked up the worn wallet from the table. He slipped it into the front pocket of his jeans.

"Tell you what I'll do, Posey. Might help you out some. I'm sending Moss into Troy after lunch to pick up a couple of prisoners at the county lockup. You can hitch a ride into town with him if you want to. He'll be driving the van. Likely the same one that delivered you to our door."

"All right," mumbled Posey. He stepped past the officer, opened the door, and strode down the hallway to freedom. Freedom as he understood it.

There was one row of seats behind the driver and then the cage where the prisoners rode. He sat on the edge of the seat behind Moss, leaning over so that he could see out of the windshield. Moss geared down as they approached the light in heavy traffic. He then saw a man standing in the median holding a sign, with *Will Work For Food* written on it in neat black letters.

"I'll get out here, Moss."

"Hell, we're a mile or more from the jailhouse."

"I'm getting off here."

"Suit yourself. Ain't no skin off my butt," said Moss as he pulled the handle, opening the door of the bus. "See you in the funny papers, Posey."

Posey did not respond, but quickly exited the bus and walked leisurely around in front of it to the median where the man with the sign stood. The light turned and the traffic surged forward. The man dropped the sign to his side and walked past him, his head down. He appeared at first to be somewhat neatly dressed, but on looking closer you could see the tear in the tee shirt and the soiled jeans that he wore. Black duct tape was wrapped around one of his dirty, tattered sneakers.

"Hey," Posey called out.

"What do you want?" The man stopped and turned toward him.

"Nothing. Just got into town. Lookin' to hook up with somebody, I reckon."

"This here corner's mine so go look someplace else."

"Hell, man, I ain't wantin' your corner. Is there a rescue mission or something around here? Somewhere to get something to eat?"

"Yeah, there might be. You sober?"

"Yeah, I'm sober."

"Take a left here." The man pointed toward the intersection. "Salvation Army's about ten blocks. But you better be sober or they won't fool with you."

"Yeah, I'm plenty sober all right," said Posey, and then he darted across the busy street, not looking back.

The light turned red and the man with the sign turned toward to the stopped traffic. He figured he'd make fifty dollars today. Same as yesterday.

Posey stood on the sidewalk facing the Salvation Army compound. To his left was the church, the chapel. Beside the chapel separated by a gated drive was the administration building, or so the sign said. Beyond the gate, which appeared to be locked, were other buildings. Dormitories maybe. The place reminded him of prison.

He sauntered across the asphalt skirt beyond the sign for the administration building and stepped up onto the small porch. He hesitated for a moment and then pushed the door open. At what appeared to be the reception desk sat a man in a clean tee shirt and jeans. He looked up at Posey as he approached.

"Can I help you?"

Posey stopped and looked around the room. There were several crosses on the wall and a painting of Jesus. On one wall were photos of men, old men, all in some kind of uniform. There was a small bronze plate on the frame beneath each picture with something written on it. He could not read them form where he stood.

"Can I help you?" repeated the man behind the desk.

Posey looked at him. "Uh, yeah. At least I hope so. I reckon I need a place to stay. I mean, just for a few days.

"You just get into town?"

"I reckon you might could say that. I've been locked up. I just got out this morning."

"Locked up, huh? Get out on parole?"

"Naw, I served my time."

"Well, that don't sound too good."

"Look, can you put me up or not. If you can't, I'll just move on."

"That all depends. I mean, if you can stay here."

"On what?"

"First, on your application. Here." The man pulled a clipboard from a desk drawer and handed it to Posey. "Fill this out and I'll have the director take a look at it." Posey took the clipboard. "You can sit over there by the window and fill it out. Won't take you but a few minutes. I assume you can read."

"I can read," said Posey, looking hard at the man. The man stared back at him. Posey sighed deeply and turned away. He walked over and sat down in a straight back chair and began to fill out the application. When he had finished it he stepped back up to the desk and handed the clipboard to the man. He took the application off the clipboard and looked at it carefully.

"Okay, just have a seat. I'll be back in a few minutes." The man got up from the desk and disappeared momentarily through a door behind him, and then came back to his desk. Posey returned to the chair and waited. After a while a man in uniform entered from the door behind the desk. The man at the desk looked up and said to Posey, "This here's the Captain."

Though the room that he shared with the other dozen or so men was much smaller, it still reminded him uncomfortably of prison. He would stay here until the end of the week. That was all he could stand, and besides, he had plans. Plans for moving on.

For the men who wanted to work there were day jobs doing menial tasks and getting paid at the end of the day—always in cash. At quitting time on Friday Posey had two-hundred fifty dollars in his pocket. The small group of men had drawn their pay for the day and walked to the bus stop on the corner.

"Hey, Turk, there's a bar down the street. C'mon, I'll buy you a beer."

"You crazy, Posey. You know you can't stay at the shelter if you been drinking."

"Hell, they'll never know. Just a couple of beers. Won't hurt nothing."

"Not me. I ain't drinking nothing. Let's go back to the shelter and get some supper."

"Naw, I ain't going back there," Posey said in a flat voice, and walked away from the group of men standing on the corner at the bus stop.

The Greyhound station was downtown, only a few blocks away. Posey went up to the ticket counter and paid the attendant forty-nine dollars for a one-way to Nashville which left at nine o'clock. In three hours. He then slumped in a seat at the far end of the terminal, pulled his cap over his eyes, and waited.

CHAPTER 12

The sun had already set when the patrol car entered the outskirts of town. In the dimming light of dusk, traffic on the highway was light and it was still too hot for many people to be out on the sidewalks, though there were some. The day had been a waste as far as he could tell except for the connections. The connection between the Boy and the two men, and them all being seen by the woman at the store, and the creek where the girl was stabbed. It figured that the two drifters, at least one of them, had killed the young woman up near Sadler's Creek and the Boy knew something or had seen something. He'd call the McBee County police when he got back to the office this evening and let them know about the trailer. At least maybe they would be on the lookout for the two men. The Boy and the woman, whoever they were, could likely be found at the bottom of the river.

As he approached the intersection the outside lights of the 7-11 came on, and the store became an illuminated island of the garish white light. He flicked the lever on the steering column to signal a left turn, but caught the glimpse of a hitchhiker up on ahead. He disengaged the turn signal and accelerated through the traffic light. You didn't see hitchhikers much anymore, not near town, and he wanted to know who was coming and going through Troy. The hitchhiker saw the police car's approach and immediately thrust his hands in his pockets and walked on. The Deputy passed by him and pulled the car up to the curb. He got out and walked back to the young boy.

"Seen you with your thumb stuck out. Where you headed, son?"

"Just up the road a ways," the Boy said, his eyes averted away from the policeman.

"Anywhere in particular?" asked the Deputy lightly.

"I ain't breakin' no laws, am I?" he Boy said, finally looking up at the Deputy.

"Not just walking down the street. But you weren't just walking down the road, now were you?" The Boy did not respond. "It's about dark besides. You best tell me who you are and what you up to."

The Boy hesitated. "I'm lookin' for my daddy."

"Your daddy, eh? He lives here somewhere around Troy or you just passing through?"

"He's around Troy, I reckon."

"Got an address for your daddy?"

"Not exactly," the Boy said softly. He bit his lower lip and looked away from the Deputy.

"Not exactly," pressed the Deputy.

"He's in jail."

"In jail. Well, maybe I *can* help you after all. What's his name?"

The Boy spoke the name of his father almost in a whisper. He was tired and scared. He only had a little of his aunt's ten dollars left. Maybe the policeman *could* help him. Just don't say too much, he told himself.

"Umm, I don't recall the name. Not in my jail anyway. That is, the county jail."

"He's on the chain gang."

"Oh, that's different. The he *is* enjoying the hospitality of the county. Unfortunately, they ain't precisely chain gangs anymore. But they do work on the roads and such.

He's—your daddy—likely down at the Burrellson Camp. It's county run."

"Where is it?" asked the Boy with interest, if not excitement, rising in his voice.

"It's down off this highway, but it's a ways from here. Don't matter, though, they wouldn't let you near the place anyhow."

"Well, I'm goin' to try just the same. I figure they got visitin' days."

"They do, on Sunday afternoons. But you ain't going anywhere. At least not until I know a little more about where you come from."

"I ain't from nowhere."

"We all from somewhere, son. Now tell me, where's your kin?"

"I ain't got no kin."

"Going to play it that way, huh?" the deputy sighed and pushed his hat back off his forward.

"Look here, boy, I'm tired and hungry and I ain't up to no foolishness," the Deputy said and he placed a hand on the Boy's shoulder. "But I'll tell what I'll do. You come on and get in my car and we'll drive over to my office. I'll call down to Burrellson and check on your daddy. In the meantime, you can tell me about yourself and where you come from. That's fair, ain't it?"

"I reckon," said the Boy. He was tired and hungry, too. It was dark now and he was as good as lost. But he had found out where his daddy was, maybe. He could make up a tale to give to the policeman. Maybe he would give him something to eat.

The Deputy walked back to the patrol car and opened the passenger side door. The Boy trudged up to the car where the he stood.

"You ever rode in a police car before?"

"No," said the Boy, disinterestedly.

"Don't matter. You can just throw your backpack there in the back seat."

The feeling surprised him when he got into the car and the Deputy pushed the door shut. As the policeman walked around the car and got in, the Boy felt a sense of relief. He then realized that he had not felt safe in a long time, and certainly not since yesterday. In his mind, his vague plan had ended when he had located his father. How his father could help him from prison he had not considered, but had felt some kind of inexplicable comfort in making the connection with someone of his own blood.

He sat in the drab room, a lobby of sorts. The Deputy had told him to wait there while he made the phone call which he did in his office. Across the room was a long glassed- in counter behind which several policemen busied themselves with paper work and answering the phones. Their voices were loud and carried the edge of bored authority. They never have to be afraid, he thought. Men with huge black guns in holsters belted tight to their waists. Cars with radios and sirens. They could do whatever they liked and no one could do anything about it. Shoot at people. Arrest people, good or bad or just because you didn't like them. I bet it's fun, he thought.

Finally, the Deputy came into the room and stood over the Boy.

"I got news for you, son, but it's not good. Not for you, anyway."

"Did you find out about my daddy?"

"Yes I did. I talked to the assistant warden down at Burrellson. Your daddy was there all right, but he's been out three or four months. Of course, they got no idea where he is. Served his time and they let him go. That's the way it works, you know."

The Boy looked up at the Deputy for a long moment then hung his head. No one will see me cry, he said to himself as tears welled in his eyes. His plan had ended here. The future did not exist for him now. Only a silent blackness from which he could not see beyond. It did not matter anymore. He knew he could trust no one.

"Okay, son. I reckon it's time you and me tend to some business. Let's go back to my office."

He led the Boy across the room, past the glassed-in counter to a door beside it. The Deputy held the door open for him and then closed it behind him.

"Take a seat," said the Deputy, pointing to a chair just in front of his desk. The Deputy went around and sat down behind the desk. The air conditioner rattled on. He propped his elbow on the desk and clasped his hands together. He rested his chin on them and looked at the Boy, who was staring down at his shoes. For a long moment neither spoke.

Finally, the boy looked up and spoke. "Why are you lookin' at me?"

The Deputy signed deeply and leaned back into his chair.

"I reckon you figured this was coming. You got folks someplace, right?"

"No," the Boy answered softly, not looking up at the Deputy. "I don't have no people."

"Well, that's hardly likely now ain't it? The sooner you tell me who you are and where you come from, the sooner I can get you back there. They'll be looking for you. So let's get on with it."

The Boy did not readily respond. He knew some things and none of them were good. He did not want to talk about it. He just wanted to run from here, from everyone. Just to be left alone. He wasn't afraid of being alone, at least he didn't think he was. Not now. Strangely, the image of the girl flashed before him. She, without the two men, standing up on the bank looking down at him. He could see the rise and fall of her breasts beneath the thin tee shirt as she breathed, looking down at him, not smiling.

"Where you live, son?" asked the Deputy, impatiently.

He knew the future was now and there would be no escape.

"Up on Sadler's Creek," he said, almost in a whisper. The words had just leapt from his mouth. His voice had surprised him.

"Sadler's Creek," repeated the Deputy, as the words and thoughts exploded in his brain. Holy shit, he thought. Is this the Boy. Could it be? For an instant, his thoughts and heart raced. The Boy held the key. He was probably scared. This could be tricky. He then became a policeman again and started to think like one.

"Sadler's Creek, huh? I believe that's somewhere over in McBee County, ain't it?"

"I reckon it is," he said softly, his head still down.

"You've come a ways, then. Hitchhiked the whole way."

"Yes."

"You ever live on River Road out past Russellville?"

"No," came the response, too quick.

"Ever live in a blue house trailer?"

"No."

The Deputy stood up and moved around to the front of the desk, leaning against it gazing down at the Boy in the chair. He folded his arms across his chest.

"So your folks live up near Sadler's Creek?"

"Yes."

"They got a phone?"

"No. No phone."

The Deputy knew he had a mess on his hands and the Boy was not telling him much. Nothing truthful anyway. It was a mixed blessing, both good and bad. He was almost certain this might be the Boy. Something had happened at the trailer that day. He was running from it, or something. He knew something about the murder. He must. But he was scared and the Deputy knew he would have to go lightly. He also felt he was getting close.

"Look, here, I tell you what we're going to do. It's late. And Sadler's Creek is a long way from here. I'm going to get us some supper and you going stay here tonight. I mean with me, not here at the jail," the Deputy chuckled briefly. "First thing in the morning we'll drive over there and get you settled back in with your folks."

"All right," replied the Boy. He knew he had no choice, but now he felt that he had bought some time to try and figure something out.

"In the meantime, we'll walk over to the Tic-Toc and get some supper. You hungry?"

"No," replied the boy softly, still looking down at his shoes.

They left the station and crossed the street. The Tic-Toc diner was another block down. It was dark by now and all the street lights had blinked on. Neither one of them spoke. When they got to the restaurant the Deputy held the glass door open and ushered the Boy inside.

The diner was cool and smelled of fried food. The air itself felt almost greasy. A long counter ran nearly the length of the room on one side, facing a row of booths on the other. The Deputy walked down between them and sat down in a booth away from the counter, but where he could see it. He motioned for the Boy to do the same and he took a seat across from him. The Deputy removed his hat and placed it beside him.

There was a man at the far end of the counter. His head was down and he seemed to be mumbling to the coffee cup that was in front of him. He had not looked up when the Deputy and the Boy entered. Other than the waitress, no one else was in the diner. She—the waitress—was behind the counter leaning against the kitchen door post. She was picking at her fingernails which were painted black. Her heavily made-up face was not pretty, but her pink uniform was unbuttoned by two more buttons than it should have been, exposing significant cleavage, and she *was* well-endowed. She looked bored and did not acknowledge the two in the booth.

So that's the new waitress, thought the Deputy. That's what all the fuss is about.

"This would be a good place for a restaurant," the Deputy finally said to her, loudly across the room.

She looked up. "You're not my table."

"Well, whose table are we?"

"Peggy's"

"Okay, I'll play along," said the Deputy sarcastically. "Would Peggy happen to be working tonight by any chance?"

"Yeah, she's working. She's out back having a smoke. Should be back directly," replied the waitress, returning to her nails.

"Look, sweetie, we don't have all night. How about taking our order, okay?"

The waitress sighed and grimaced, and then walked over to the counter, leaning on it toward the booth where they sat.

Damn, thought the Deputy as he over looked at her. She's going to come out of that dress. She continued to lean over, exposing herself as much as possible. She held an order pad and pencil in her hands, resting on the counter.

"Okay, what'll it be?"

"I'll make this real easy for you," answered the Deputy. "Bring us a couple of burgers well-done. With some fries. I'll have coffee. Bring the kid here a Coke."

"We don't have Coke."

"Well, then just bring him whatever it is you do have."

"Pepsi."

"Okay, bring him a Pepsi then."

"All right," she said and sauntered of toward the kitchen.

The Boy had folded his arms on the table and had lain his head on them. The Deputy looked over at him and finally said, "Tired out, are you?"

"I'm a little tired," answered the Boy, holding his head up and sitting erect.

"Say you from up around Sadler's Creek, huh?"

"That's right."

"You know something?"

"What?"

"It just so happens I was up at Sadler's Creek recently."

"So?"

"Well, the truth of the matter is I didn't see any houses around there. Looked pretty much like wilderness to me. That is except for the store there at the corner of the dirt road and the highway. You know the one I'm talking about?" The Boy didn't respond.

Just then another waitress, Peggy, arrived at the booth with a tray of food.

"Out kinda late, ain't you, deputy?"

"Oh, hello, Peggy. Seem to be working late yourself."

She placed the food on the table. "I suppose you get the Pepsi," she said to the Boy."

"Yes, ma'am."

"Yeah, I'm pulling a double shift. Connie Rae called in sick again."

"Looks like you got some real good back-up though," said the Deputy, nodding toward the large-breasted woman behind the counter.

"Now don't get me started," said Peggy. She shook her head. "Y'all need anything else right now?"

"No, we're fine. Might bring me a warm-up when you come back this way."

"Will do," she answered and walked away.

When the Deputy turned back toward him, the Boy had nearly devoured the burger and was stuffing French fries in his mouth.

"Weren't hungry, huh," chucked the Deputy.

The Boy did not respond as he reached for his glass and gulped down the Pepsi.

Ordinarily, he would have called the sheriff over in McBee County and had them come get the Boy, hand the problem over to them and be done with it. This would likely eventually happen, but not just yet. He, too, needed some time. He wanted to find the low-life he had been chasing, at least in his mind, for months. He was too close to have the McBee County sheriff bungle the case. He would, with the Boy, drive up to the store in the morning. The woman there would know it when she saw him. He'd get a positive ID. The kid would tell him what he knew or what he had seen on the creek and what had happened at the trailer—maybe. Then he'd be McBee County's problem. He was just stretching procedure a tad. That's all. Shouldn't be a problem.

CHAPTER 13

Posey was roused from a shallow sleep by the dispatcher announcing the nine o'clock boarding. He sat up, push his cap back on his head. He looked down at the ticket sticking out of his shirt pocket and touched it. Nashville, Tennessee. He stood up slowly and sauntered into the Men's Room. Placing the cap beside the sink, he splashed cold water on his face. He then brushed back his hair with both wet hands and glanced up into the mirror, and smiled at himself. Not bad for thirty-eight. Not bad, at least for the life he had led. He'd do all right in Nashville.

He walked out of the bathroom, across the dingy terminal, out the glass doors and onto the bus. He made his way toward the rear, passing the few ne'er-do-wells already seated. Like him, he thought, except most of them were black. But that was okay. He had money in his pocket and was finally getting the hell out of Wofford County. He was on the big grey dog, and by tomorrow morning he'd be in Nashville. He took a seat by the window and stretched out partially on the seat beside him which was empty. The bus roared and lumbered away from the terminal, turned down Main, heading for Interstate 49. For a few moments, Posey gazed out the window. Downtown Troy, other than for a few street lights, was mostly dark this time of night. Nothing but small-town nobodies, he said to himself. Hicks and losers. He then slumped in his seat, He pulled the cap down over his face and fell into a deep sleep.

Posey had not woke when the bus pulled off the Interstate and into the Atlanta station. There was a change of drivers and the passengers waiting in the terminal began to board. Posey sat up in his seat and straightened his cap.

"Shit! We're only in Atlanta," he said to himself as he gazed out the window, looking at the stream of people boarding the bus. He could see the terminal sign and the large clock in the station. A quarter past one. The bus was going to be full, or close to it.

A tall, thin black man wearing a beret made his way down the aisle, passing several empty seats. He stopped at Posey.

"Mind if I sit here?" he said and he lifted the brown paper bag he carried into the overhead bin.

"It's a free country," said Posey, glancing up. And then turning away. He did not like black people.

"Well, some say it is and some say it ain't," said the black man as he settled in the seat beside Posey.

"I reckon."

The black man suddenly sat up. "You *reckon*! Man, you sound like you straight from the sticks. *I reckon*," he repeated and laughed. "A real cracker."

Posey tensed and clinched his fist. "You some uppity nigger, out here in the middle of the night

126

riding a bus with everything you own in a grocery sack."

"Who you calling a nigger?"

"Who you calling a cracker?"

"Hell, I ain't sitting here," said the black man angrily as he rose from the seat and reached up for his bag. "I sure ain't sitting with no cracker-ass honky!" He moved away up toward the front of the bus, pushing aside other people in the aisle. Posey folded his arms and slumped in the seat, pulling his cap back down over his eyes. They'd be back on the road shortly, headed north, he reminded himself.

"Hey," came the thin voice as he felt someone sit down in the seat beside him. Posey pushed back the cap and looked over at the boy.

"Hey," he replied dully.

"We going to Nashville," said the boy.

"That a fact?"

"Yes, sir, it sure is. My daddy sent for us. We going to live with him. Be a family again."

Posey looked beyond the boy, across the aisle as a woman was situating herself and a small, sleeping baby in the seat. She glanced over at him.

"You don't mind if my boy sits there do you, mister?" she asked wearily.

"No, ma'am."

"All right. Kenny you behave yourself and don't bother that nice man. We still got a long way to go. Go to sleep."

"All right, I'll try," said the boy, but he was wide awake and too excited to sleep.

The bus was finally loaded and pulled out of the station, winding its way through the city streets headed for the north-bound Interstate. It eventually found the ramp and roared onto the highway. The boy was nowhere near sleep. He looked over at the man beside him.

"You going all the way to Nashville too?" he asked Posey.

"Yeah, I reckon I am."

"I can't wait to get there. We're going to see my daddy. I mean, we're going to live with him."

"You already told me that."

"He's been working in Nashville. He plays guitar in a band."

"That's nice."

"He's been trying to make it. You know, with a band. He's a good guitar player. He can sing too." Posey looked at the boy, but then turned away and stared into the darkness beyond the window. "Do you live in Nashville or you just visiting?" the boy continued.

Posey hesitated and sighed. "I'm going there to live."

"Maybe I'll see you there."

"I doubt it."

"I guess we'll see. Daddy's got us a place already. Near town, he said. What you going to do in Nashville?"

"You know something, sonny? You ask too many questions," said Posey and he then turned away from the boy, toward the window.

Rebuked, and sitting awake in the darkness of the bus, the boy looked around him. His mother was a dark form across the aisle holding the infant. Both were asleep. He then glanced over at the man sitting beside him.

"Mister, I'm sorry I bugged you. Didn't mean to. I just get worked up sometimes. I'll try not to talk no more, but I bet if you had a kid like me, you'd understand."

Posey opened his eyes in the darkness. If I had a kid like you, he thought. Without looking at the boy he answered, softly, almost to himself, "But I don't."

CHAPTER 14

The cruiser slowed and turned off the state highway onto the county road that would take them through Russellville and then the few miles to the store. The Deputy hadn't said much, but glanced occasionally over at the Boy while he drove. The Boy was glad that there had been no more questions. He thought the Deputy slow and stupid.

He looked up ahead and on the left in the distance was where the Preacher's camper has been parked. What the Preacher had done or tried to do did not bother him much now. At least he didn't get baptized. The Preacher was just stupid too. That's all.

As they road approached the field where he had spent the night with the Preacher, he glanced cautiously at it, half expecting to see the car and the camper, and maybe the Preacher himself. But it was all gone. Instead, a carnival had moved in. Carnies were erecting the rides and game booths, and spreading what looked to be sawdust on the ground. It all looked sad, dilapidated and squalid in the early afternoon sun. Still, as the car passed, he kept his gaze on the seedy collection of tents and the faded painted steel and the faceless people until it all shrank and disappeared from his view.

"Ever been to a carnival?" asked the Deputy

"Just a circus. Once, a long time ago."

"Pretty sorry looking bunch back there. Probably looks okay at night when they turn the lights up. Kind of like it ain't real," the Deputy chuckled, "I mean at night."

The Boy did not respond. But he was thinking about the carnival. What it must be like. It looked all right to him in the daylight, but he would like to see it at night. With the lights. And what it felt like. A carnival, traveling and staying on the road, might be a good life. No one knowing or caring who you were or where you came from. Always moving. New places all the time. He hadn't been to a carnival, but he would sure like to. No connections there. The plan to find his father had been stupid, he thought. So I'm stupid too. Trying to make a connection with someone was a silly idea. He wasn't connected to anyone and never would be. He didn't really know what a connection was or what it felt like. Were the thoughts he had about the girl something like a connection. It had felt strange to him, but strange in a warm, good way. It made no sense. Best he just forget about it.

"I reckon all this around here looks pretty familiar to you," the Deputy said once they were through Russellville.

"I know where I am," the said sullenly. He had fought hard with himself not to think about what was going to happen to him once it was obvious to the Deputy that he didn't live up here and that he'd lied. The system would take over, he knew that. And he knew what that meant for him. It was bad and it was inevitable, so why bother worrying about it. Just play it out.

As the car pulled onto the gravel and stopped beside the inept and rusting gas pumps, he sat up straighter in the seat. He looked over at the store and could see through the screen door the outline of the woman perched on the stool inside, behind the counter.

"Let's go inside for minute, okay" the Deputy said with a slight grin, but the Boy knew he wasn't asking, so he got out of the car and followed him into the store.

"Well, well, sheriff, you gettin' to be one of my regulars. Want one all-the-way, same as before?" she said, with the ubiquitous cigarette dangling from her lips.

"I reckon not. I'm here on business."

"Official po-lice business?"

"I reckon as official as I can be over here in McBee County." The Boy stood behind the Deputy and she had not yet gotten a good look at him.

"Is that one of your new men there behind you? A rookie maybe. He's a mite short, ain't he?" her laugh was interrupted by a hoarse cough. She cleared her throat and took a drag off the cigarette.

"Come on around here, son," the Deputy said. He turned and grasp the Boy by his shoulder.

The woman slid off the stool and leaned forward with both elbows on the counter, her eyes darting back on forth between the Deputy and the Boy. She took the cigarette from her mouth, pinching it gently between her thumb and forefinger.

"Well, I be damned. You found him. I ain't believing this!" she exclaimed and slapped the counter top with an open palm.

"He the one?" asked the Deputy.

"Either it is or his identical twin. You a Redden, ain't you, boy," she declared.

"No, I don't think..."

"I ain't no Redden!" the Boy said, interrupting the Deputy.

"Well, you sure look like one."

"But I ain't."

"No, I reckon you ain't at that."

"That's what I suspected. Found him hitchhiking over near Troy. Damnest thing. Pure luck I found him like I did."

"Might be bad luck, sheriff," warned the woman. "He know anything about that young woman gettin' killed?"

The Deputy grimaced at the woman's question and shot her a quick look of warning and exasperation.

"We ain't had time to talk yet. I had to see if he was the one you saw that day."

"What woman?" the Boy asked nervously. He was thinking about his aunt. Maybe they thought he had killed her.

"Why, that girl up on Sadler's Creek. Time they say she was killed was about the time I seen you go off fishing up there."

"All right, both of you hush," the Deputy turned to the Boy. "You were fishing on the creek?"

"I didn't kill nobody."

"No one's accusing you of anything, but we need to talk. I got some questions. Maybe you can help me, or me you."

"I didn't kill nobody. I didn't kill no girl."

"Look, you go on out there and wait in the car. I'll be out directly," said the Deputy.

"All right," the Boy said, the screen door slammed shut behind him as he left the store.

They both watched him walk across the gravel yard and get into the patrol car. He slumped into the seat, his head barely visible.

"Like I told you before," said the woman, "kinda snooty."

"The Boy's in a mess of trouble. Maybe more than he knows. I don't know what he saw, but I aim to find out. I just had to make sure he was the one what came in here that morning."

"Ain't no doubt about it. That's the kid. You going to take him back over to Wofford County? I mean, since you don't know where he lives and all."

"I might know where he *was* staying, but that ain't my concern just now."

"Well, he's the one," she said as she sat back on the stool.

"Anybody else been nosing around since I was last up here?"

"No strangers, if that's what you mean."

"Sheriff from McBee County?"

"Nope." She crushed what was left of the cigarette in the ash tray.

"Well, them ole boys down there in Corinth about to be up to their necks in this trouble."

"Whatcha mean"? she asked as she took the last cigarette from the pack and lit it. She crumbled up the empty pack and dropped it into the wastebasket under the counter.

"Nothing that concerns you, I don't reckon. I've done said too much," he said.

"I don't give a damn either way. I don't need the trouble."

The Deputy turned and walked back to the drink cooler and pulled two bottles from the icy water.

"Reckon I'll get me and the Boy a drink," he said, placing two dripping bottles of Tom's Orange and money on the counter. The woman made change. "Don't expect I'll be back up this way, 'least not anytime soon."

"Hope you find what you lookin' for, sheriff."

"Deputy," he said dryly.

"Whatever. When you get to hankerin' for a good hotdog, which you will sooner or later, come on back up and see me," she leaned back on the stool with her arms folded across he breast, the cigarette dangling from her fingers.

"They got hotdogs over in Troy," he said good naturedly.

"Yeah, I'm sure they do, but not like mine."

The Deputy grinned and nodded his head slightly.

"Anyway, thanks for your help. I mean in identifying the Boy."

He left the store and walked to the car. The Boy was still slumped in the seat, staring through the windshield at the road beyond which eventually curved out of sight. The Deputy passed one of the soft drinks to him. He took it without acknowledgement.

"Wouldn't' kill you to say thank you, would it?" asked the Deputy.

"Thanks," mumbled the Boy with equal sarcasm.

"We going to ride up that dirt road there up to Sadler's Creek and have a look around. Maybe you can tell me who or what you saw that day."

"I didn't see nothing," the Boy said. He did not look at the Deputy.

"Well, maybe you did and maybe you didn't. Maybe just looking around up there you'll remember something."

"I won't," the Boy said sullenly.

"Well, then, you can show me where you went fishing. You can do that, can't you?"

"I reckon."

"And where you live?" The Boy didn't respond.

The patrol car made a U-turn in the gravel lot in front of the store and turned left onto the dirt road. The afternoon sun was passing quickly, casting lengthening shadows which tunneled the road as they drove. Clouds of red dust boiled up behind the vehicle. Finally, the car slowed as the Deputy spotted a sign up ahead and a narrow bridge beyond it.

"Sign says 'Sadler's Creek'," said the Deputy as he pulled the car over to the side of the road. "This here where you go fishing?"

"Near here," replied the Boy softly.

"That day?"

"Yeah," the Boy said, and hesitated. "That day."

With the engine idling, the Deputy gripped the steering wheel and looked down at the Boy beside him, pressed against the passenger-side door.

"Look here, son, the sooner we do this, the sooner we can get out of here. I'm trying to find two nasty bums, drifters I reckon. They're killers and I think you know some things. Just show me where you went fishing that day. That's all."

"Then what?" the Boy asked, turning to look into the Deputy's face.

"Well, I ain't going to lie to you. I got to take you down to Corinth. To the sheriff's office down there. This is their deal now. Look, I been to that trailer where you live out on River Road. Something's bad took place out there, but I don't figure you going to tell me anything about it. That is, if you know anything."

The Boy wasn't thinking about the trailer, or his aunt, or the two men down at the river. He was thinking about being taken to the sheriff's office in Corinth. It didn't matter whether or not he told the police what he had seen or if they found the killers. The result for him was the same. They'd call the department of social services in and he'd be held there until they put him in another foster home. The beatings, the abuse, the drunk men—these memories all came flooding back to him, not dream-like but intense and vivid. The smells filled his nostrils even now. This will never happen to me again, he had repeated to himself.

"The police in Corinth?" the Boy asked, preoccupied and distant.

"Sure. You'll be safe there. They'll find your folks. You'll be fine."

But there were no folks and he figured the Deputy suspected this by now. He just wanted information and then he'd be through with him. The fear of the two men was nothing compared to his dread of what the system would do to him. It won't happen, he again promised himself.

"There's a path other side of those bushes. Goes down to the creek. That's where I started fishing."

"Good. Real good. Now you're cooperating. No need to be afraid." The Deputy reached over and removed a large black flashlight from the glove compartment. "Light's starting to fade. Might need this before we get back to the car. Come on, let's go."

The Boy opened the door slowly and got out of the car. The Deputy was already standing in the road. The Boy, with his hands jammed into the pocket of his jeans, walked past him toward the creek.

"This way," he said, and the Deputy followed.

As he strode into the woods toward the creek, with the Deputy following a few yards behind, the Boy forced himself to think. He'd show him the creek and where he had fished that day, which now seemed long ago and was no longer clear in his mind. Except for the girl who had stopped smiling when she had looked down at him from the bank. He remembered watching the movement of her breasts beneath the thin tee shirt as she breathed. And his skin feeling hotter and the sun itself beating down on him. He did not understand why this memory was so vivid, so sharply focused in his mind, but it was. He did not mind it.

I'll show him the creek and then the Deputy will take me down to Corinth. The policeman there at the desk will look at me, scratch his head, and then pick up the phone and call social services. They'd come get me right off no matter what time it was; it will be late by then. Protective Services, they'll tell me and I know what that means. They'll know who I am right off and ask me about my aunt. I won't tell them nothing; all *that* trouble will come later. I'll go to the dorm or some house they got full of other losers like me. Then into a foster home as quick as they can find one. I'll never go back to a foster home, he repeated to himself. He'd have to get away from this dumb-ass deputy. Somehow. Then he suddenly found himself at the edge of the creek and stopped.

"How much further?" the Deputy called from behind him. He did not respond. Finally, the Deputy walked up beside him, breathing heavily. He pulled a handkerchief from his pocket and wiped his face.

"This here's the creek, eh?"

"Yeah, this is the creek," the Boy answered matter of factly.

"This where you saw 'em?"

"I never said I saw anybody."

"But is this where you fished?"

"No, it was down a ways," the Boy gestured with a thin finger. "I'll show you."

The Boy turned quickly and headed off into the woods that bordered the creek downstream as the Deputy was still catching his breath.

"Whoa, wait up, son," he called, but the Boy had disappeared into the gloom of the forest.

The Deputy finally caught up with him. He found the Boy standing on the bank near the stream.

"This is where I went in."

"Went in?"

"Yeah, you know, I was wadin'. That's the way you catch trout. You got to get in the water."

"Okay. So you entered here and started fishing. Is this where you saw them?"

"I never told you I saw anything."

"But you did, didn't you?"

"I saw some people," the Boy said finally.

"Here?"

"No, more on down the creek."

"Okay, before we go on down there tell me who, or what, you saw that day."

"It wasn't nothing much. Just two men, both about drunk, and a girl. A woman, I guess."

"Did they see you?"

"Yeah, they saw me."

"Did you talk to them?"

"Some, I reckon, but I didn't want to."

"What did they say? To you, I mean."

"Nothing much. Just that they were going up across the creek and have a party. Something like that. They were drunk. The girl too, I reckon."

"We're they forcing the women to go with them?"

The boy looked out across the creek and thought about that day, the day he had seem her standing on the back above him, looking down at him, not smiling. Finally, he turned to the Deputy.

"No, they weren't forcing her to do anything. She was drinkin' too."

"So you got a look at them?"

"Yeah, I got a look at the them."

"A good look?"

"A real good look."

The Deputy started to ask the Boy about his aunt, but decided not to. Not yet. He had gotten him this far and he'd finish this part out. There would be time to talk later.

"Okay, show me where you saw the two men and the woman."

"All right," replied the boy. "Just follow me." And he the darted into the trees along the bank of the stream.

As soon as he was out of sight of the Deputy he began to run and run hard. He knew that if he stayed near the bank he could find the path. The secret path, he thought, that led back to the dirt road. He could be gone before the Deputy realized he was fleeing. By the time the policeman got out of the woods and back to his car it would be dark and he would be on his way.

But on his way where? Then he remembered the carnival they had driven by just outside of Russellville. He wanted to see it at night. He wanted to see it all lit up at night. There would be people there. All strangers. That was good. He could get lost among them. Carnivals did not stay in one place very long. They moved around. He knew that. Maybe he could hang around and leave with them. Maybe he could work at the carnival. Maybe even travel with the carnival. Then they'd would never find him. Maybe the carnival would become some kind of connection for him. It seemed like a dream to him at first. But as he ran through the darkening woods it began to seem real somehow. Maybe it *was* possible. He had to try, he knew that much.

CHAPTER 15

The fire crackled and blazed up when the Small man dropped a handful of dry, dead pine limbs onto it. He then resumed his position on the ground, leaning on a piece of dead tree trunk he had dragged out of the surrounding woods and placed near the fire. The Big man stood opposite him, gazing into the flames.

"She sunk real good, didn't she?" said the Big man. It was not a question that he really intended to be answered.

"What with all them cement blocks tied to her, I reckon she did. River looked deep, too Dropped down right off at the bank."

"Deep enough, I'd say. They won't be no easy time findin' her."

"Nope, they won't."

After rolling the weighted body off the bank into the river the two men had trudged back up the bare, steep hill to the trailer to wait for the Boy. For a while they both sat on the low makeshift bench in the trailer yard, with hollow eyes staring blankly and obtusely at the ground. Thunder rumbled in the distance. Pointed shadows of the tall oak trees behind the trailer began to creep across the dirt yard toward them as the sun angled westward.

"Kid orta been here by now. Ain't no school holdin' this late," said the Small man.

The Big man glanced across at the trailer door.

"Don't reckon he come while we was down at the river?"

"You thinkin' he might be inside? I ain't heard nothin'."

"Come to think of it, I reckon that front door was shut when we drug her off. Looky yonder. That goddamn rod and reel's a-layin' on the ground!"

"Damned if it ain't!"

They quickly entered the trailer and moved swiftly from room to room, slamming doors, knocking over lamps and the contents of shelves to the floor. There did not seem to be a clue as to whether the Boy had been there.

"Might have come and gone," the Small man called from the Boy's room. "The drawers are all pulled out and they's a pile of school books in the middle of the floor."

The Big man stepped into the small bedroom and surveyed the disarray.

"That little sumbitch has come and gone, sure as hell!"

"Reckon he seen us down at the river?"

"I reckon he did. Saw us and hauled ass. But I don't figger he coulda got far. Likely headed up the road there."

"Reckon where he'd go? I can't see that old man up the road hepin' him. Woman said they ain't got no kin."

"His daddy's over on Troy, in the pen. She said that."

"That don't do us no good. I sure as hell ain't goin' nowhere near Troy!" the Small man said adamantly.

"Maybe he's just runnin' or hidin' out somewhere in these woods. But I'm figurin' he ain't got nowhere to go but to Troy."

"I ain't seein' it and ain't no way I'm lookin' for him back that a way. Let's git the hell out of here and git on up to Munro County," said the Small man, almost pleading.

"We goin' find the Boy. He done seen us twice now. Po-lice see him wanderin' around they'll pick him up. That ain't goin' be no good for me ner you."

"What are you suggestin'?"

"Reckon we'll hang around here for a while. If he's hidin' back in them woods he's likely to come back here once he thinks we gone."

"I don't know. I don't like stayin' here, with what we done and all."

"I'm goin' see if there's more beer in the ice box. Ye look around and see if ye can find some cigarettes. They's some cans of food in the kitchen cabinet. I might just bed down in the old gal's room. Bed looked like it might be right comfy."

"You figurin' on stayin' here the night?"

"I reckon I am," answered the Big man.

The two men, haggard and desperate, stayed at the trailer for a couple of days, but the Boy never returned. The Small man, restless and whiny, continued to press his loathsome accomplice to flee back to North Carolina and to the safe haven, as he saw it, of his relatives there. The Big man was sullen and unresponsive. He had resolved with what was now an inexplicable obsession to find and destroy the Boy. As with most desperate men on the run, risks had become almost irrelevant to him. He didn't fear the Law, he just didn't consider it. Finally, he coldly looked up into the Small man's face standing over him and spoke.

"I need to time to figger things out. But we goin' git that kid." He rose from the dingy soiled sheets of the bed and went into the kitchen. What was left of the can goods he placed in a brown paper grocery bag. The Small man followed him.

"What?" he asked.

"You right about one thing. We got to git out of here. I'm goin' back up in them woods up near that creek.

Nobody'll be lookin' for us up there. Not now. You comin'?"

"I reckon so," replied the Small man. "What the hell else can I do?"

It was dusk when they reached the dirt road that ran beside the store, up to Sadler's Creek. Nearing a gully, they hunched over with hands on their knees, breathing hard.

"Damn, the store's still open. They's light on," said the Small man.

"Yeah, so what?"

"I could sure drank a beer or two, that's what."

"You got shit for brains, ye know that. We don't need to be foolin' around that store and that nosey bitch what runs it. We layin' low, remember?"

"I don't think she ever saw me. Not real good anyway. I could jis' slip in there and git us some beers. Wouldn't hurt nothin' way I see it."

"We ain't goin' do it. Now let's get up the road here. C'mon," the Big man said and he started up the dirt road, in the shadows away from the store. The Small man stared wistfully at the lighted store building for a moment. Wiping his mouth with the back of his hand, he sighed, and then turned to follow his companion.

He bent over and reached into the paper bag on the ground beside the log and took out a can of beans. He pulled back the ringed tab, opened the can, and stared stupidly at its contents.

"Ain't no spoons in the sack. How the hell am I supposed to eat these beans?"

The Big man stepped over to where he sat and took the can from him. He then detached the lid, bent it back on itself. He strode back to where he had been standing over the fire and began scooping the beans into his mouth.

"Damn!" said the Small man. He then reached down again into the paper bag and withdrew another can of beans. He aped the actions of his confederate and formed a crude spoon with the metal lid. He sat, leaning against the piece of rotting log.

The Big man suddenly looked up, still slowly chewing a mouthful of beans, into the woods behind where the Small man sat.

"What is it? You hear something?"

"Shut up!"

The dirt road curved near their camp, but then turned away two or three hundred yards through the woods beyond. The Big man had caught a flicker of lights through the trees. Then the muffled sound of the engine.

"Damn car comin' down that dirt road," said the Big man.

The Small man leaned forward and placed the can on the ground. "Stomp that fire out!"

"They can't see nothin' through all them trees. Just be quiet."

As the Deputy drove slowly down the dirt road he had been scanning the woods with the spotlight mounted on the door post of the patrol car. There had been no sign of the boy as darkness had engulfed the forest. He'd come back in the morning after talking with the boys down in Corinth. The Boy would have to turn up somewhere. Maybe he was headed back to the trailer. He'd check there too. He switched off the spotlight.

As he rounded the curve something caught his eye. A flicker of light off in the otherwise dark woods to his left. He stopped the car and dimmed the headlights. The distant light beyond him in the woods continued to flicker. Damn kid's built a camp fire, he thought. Good. Real good. He pressed down the emergency brake with his foot and grabbed the flashlight from the seat beside him. He got out of the vehicle, leaving the motor idling. He flicked on the flashlight and made his way through the trees toward the small, dancing yellow light in the dark distance.

The two men had not moved. Still leaning against the dead log, the Small man stared into the fire, his ears fiercely attuned for sound. Opposite him near the fire, the Big man had spotted the car lights on the road through the trees and continued to focus on them. He had seen them dimmed, but said nothing to his companion whose back was to the road. He then saw the distant but distinct swaying beam of the flashlight approaching.

"Somebody's comin' in from the road," he said calmly.

"Shit!" whispered the Small man. "I told you we ort to git out of here. Our luck's bound to run out."

"Shut up!"

The Big man watched as the light approached. He stepped across to the edge of the clearing toward where the light was approaching. He moved into the shadows, out of the glare of the fire. He waited, the can of beans still in his hand.

The Deputy proceeded slowly but steadily as he waved the flashlight in short strokes on the ground before him. The crunch of the dry twigs and leaves seemed inordinately loud beneath his shoes. He hoped the Boy was tired and would not run. If he was going to, he would already be gone he reckoned. The Big man moved slightly toward the fire's dim light.

"Howdy, there," said the Big man as the Deputy's features grew visible in the dim shadowy light of the fire. He raised the flashlight a little, but did not point it directly in his face.

"Howdy. What you doing up here in the woods like this?"

Both of the killers could make out that the man with the flashlight was in uniform. The Small man sitting on the dead tree trunk slipped into the shadows beyond the fire. He had not been seen by the Deputy, nor had he made a sound.

"Oh, I'm jis passin' through, sheriff."

"Passing through to where?"

"Trying to git up to Hick'ry Mountain. I hear'd they's work at the saw mill up there. I shore need work, down on my luck as I am."

"Hickory Mountain, eh?"

"Yes siree. Hope to git work at the saw mill up there. Ort to be able to make it sometimes tomorrow, you reckon?"

"I don't know. You traveling by yourself?" The Deputy asked.

"Yeah, jis me. Ain't got no woman or nothing like that. I travel light."

"I see you do at that," the Deputy said with slight sarcasm. "What's that there you holding?"

"Why, this here's jis be my supper I was eatin' when I seen you a comin' through the woods. Kin I offer you some? They jis cold beans, but I got a good bit."

"You seen anybody come by?"

"Way up here in these woods?" The Big man laughed. "Reckon I ain't."

"Then you ain't seen a boy wandering around, a scrawny kid about maybe thirteen or fourteen?"

"Like I said, ain't seen nobody, kid or otherwise. You lookin' for a young'un at night up in these woods, I 'spect he's in a heap of trouble."

"Maybe," said the Deputy dryly.

"What makes ye think he'd be in these woods? Ain't nobody appears to live way off up here, not that I seen least ways."

"He's around here," said the Deputy, glancing off into the darkness.

"Can't see too good in the dark, but looks like ye shoulder patch there says Wofford County."

"That's right."

"Might git over that way one of these days. Ain't they a right good size town over there? Troy, ain't it?"

"County seat. You ever been to Troy?" the Deputy asked curiously.

"Naw. Naw, can't say I have. That boy ye lookin' fer, he from over that way?"

"Say you traveling alone, mister?" the Deputy asked, ignoring the Big man's question.

"That's right. Jis trying to git to Hick'ry Mountain, like I said. Got work up there."

As he passed light back and forth across the campsite the beam illuminated the dead fallen tree trunk. The Big man glanced back over his shoulder. Just as he had calculated, the Small man had vanished.

"You usually have supper with yourself?"

"I ain't getting' your meanin', sheriff."

Again, the Deputy slowly directed the beam across the ground to the dead tree. There on the ground was the open can of beans. The Big man's dead eyes had remained focused on the policeman.

"Seems there's another open can of something over there by that log. Strange a man traveling alone would open two cans at once, ain't it?"

The Big man dropped the can from his hand. It hit the ground in the darkness with a dull thud.

CHAPTER 16

The path, he knew, came out on the dirt road far down from the creek. He finally found his way through the trees and the bush and stood at the road's edge. He wandered if the Deputy was still back up at the creek or if he had already driven past. He had not heard any sounds of the patrol car from the woods so probably he was still back there looking for him. Don't matter, he thought.

He sat down in the pine needles to catch his breath and rest for a moment. He felt in his pocket for the few dollar bills and change that he left. Still there. It was too dark to count how much he had, but at least he had some. He was suddenly aware that he was very hungry and his throat burned with thirst. There would be no food anytime soon, he knew, but maybe he could get some water from the spigot behind the store when he got to the end of the dirt road. He hoped that the store would be closed for the night. Then the woman would be gone. He could not let her see him no matter what. She'd call the police sure as hell.

He stood up and began walking along the edge of the road, frequently glancing back over his shoulder listening, and looking for the headlights of the patrol car. But there remained only the deep blackness and silence of the forest.

He walked on until finally up ahead in the distance he saw the lights of cars flashing by. The county road. But he could not yet make out the store. As he grew closer, he saw it bathed in the dim yellow glow of the pole-mounted yard light. The building itself sat there like a huge block of black granite. There were no cars in the parked out front or anywhere else that he could see. No light shone in the store windows. The store was closed and he waited a long moment before making his way across the dirt road. He spotted the spigot. Before drinking he glanced around the yard, moving his head in quick, jerky movements. Like a small, alert animal would do. He moved into the shadow of the building. When he saw that he was safe and totally alone he knelt at the spigot and gulped down the water. He splashed it on his dust-caked face and felt the coolness as the wetness spread down his neck onto his body. The tee shirt, already wet from his sweat, stuck to his skin.

He stood and stepped to the edge of the light. He pulled the money from his pocket and counted it. Four dollars and seventy-three cents. Not much, but maybe enough, he thought. How much would it cost to get into the carnival? Something probably, but maybe nothing. All he had to do was to make it to Russellville in time and not get caught. He walked over to the county road and started down it.

As he trudged through the hot darkness he began to feel a strangeness come over him. He felt outside his own body somehow. The bad things that had happened—what he'd seen with his own eyes—over the past few days seemed to be drifting away and unreal. Maybe nothing had happened at all and he was in the midst of a heavy, black dream. Like those he had on nights not so long ago after the man who was not his real father was drunk and beat him and the others, and crushed out his cigarettes on his arms and legs.

He knew then, suddenly, that there was no rightness to the world or to him. It was all slanted and he was slanted too. And it could not be straightened and he could not be straightened, only just be there. Without connection there was nothing. It was like it was all turned inside out. He felt turned inside out. Could a dream make you feel or think like this? He lightly touched his forearm with his fingers to feel the small scars. They were still there and it was almost reassuring. It did happen. It was real.

He wondered what time it was. Almost no cars passed him on the road now so he knew it was late. I won't make it to the carnival in time tonight, he thought. Exhaustion begin to weigh on him, pressing down like a giant, black hand against his body. The energy and strength of youth had deserted him. His hunger hurt and gnawed in his gut, but he knew he needed rest. The water he had drunk from the store's spigot had revived him for a while, but it was gone. His desire to make it to the carnival had kept him going and was still burning within him, but he could not make it there. Not tonight. He walked on.

The moon, not full but bright enough as it broke sluggishly through high, bleak clouds and he could see about him clearly for the first time since dusk. Across the narrow road a low barbed-wire fence, rusting and slack, ran along the shoulder. Beyond, well away from the road, was a building—a shack—gray and slanted. One corner of it, having slipped from its support of river rocks, almost touching the ground. A small structure, maybe a barn, was beyond it sitting in an open field overgrown with sedge and kudzu. He crossed the shimmering moon-lit road and pushing down the top strand of barbed-wire, managed to get over the fence.

Nothing stirred as he approached the shack. All of the window panes had long since been broken out and nearly all the planks of what was left of the porch had rotted and fallen through. He could easily see that it was deserted. He glanced over at the small barn a few yards away. It looked to be in better repair so he crept past the house across what probably once was a chicken yard or a narrow spit of pasture. The narrow door was shut and seemed to be hanging securely on rusty hinges. When he pulled it open he was startled by a sudden loud fluttering noise and high pitch squeaking, almost screams. He jumped back from the door and started to run, but then saw the bats streak from the barn into the night sky. They flitted overhead for a moment and then disappeared into the darkness.

The opened door allowed some of the reflected light of the moon to faintly illuminate the interior and there were wide gaps in the board siding which, too, allowed in the thin lunar rays. He could make out two narrow stalls inside. He stepped in, feeling his way. The first stall contained something, a black pile, which he could not make out in the darkness. He bent over and pressed it with the open palms of his hands. A cracking and crunch came as the material gave way from his push. Corn husks. He grasped the center post to steady himself. He looked in the second stall. A shaft of moon light danced on the straw heaped in the enclosure. He wiped his knuckles across his dry lips and lay down on the straw. He considered that there were likely rats or maybe a corn snake somewhere beneath him, but these things seemed inconsequential to him now. He lay on his side, with his arms as a pillow between his head and the rough dry straw. As the moon was once again swallowed up by the slow-moving clouds, he fell into a deep, but not dreamless sleep.

For a moment he just leans against the tall tulip poplar and is mesmerized by the water. It is a wide, roaring stream strewn with boulders, some very large, protruding from the water. The pristine water splashes against and up over them, sending spray almost to the low banks on either side. Hugging up against the big rocks on the downstream side were pools, green and still and deep, where huge trout hang facing upstream, almost motionless. The beautiful carnivorous fish only move slightly to their left or right to gulp down a passing mayfly nymph caught helplessly in the current.

He raises the rod—just a wisp of bamboo— and gives it a couple of flicks in the air above his head, the cork handle feeling smooth and warm in his hand. As he steps off the bank into the shallow water it swirls about his ankles and he becomes a part of the stream. He will try a dry fly today. Much more challenging, but worth the effort and patience to see the brightly colored fish explode from beneath, through the surface of the water, and attack it. The fishing here is perfect. The water is wide and rushing, with many deep pools. There are no branches of trees overhead to interfere with his casting. And there are hungry fish everywhere. It is perfect.

He wades out to the middle of the stream, well below a deep, still pool. He whips the rod above him smoothly and rhythmically, letting out more line each time. As the rod comes forward on the last stroke, the green line falls gracefully onto the water's surface in a straight line in front of him. The fly affixed to the leader sits up still, and floats majestically in the middle of the placid pool. No trout can resist the temptation.

Suddenly the water in the pool explodes and the fly disappears. The line goes taunt instantly, bending the rod in a precarious loop. I must work this fish and not lose him, he thinks, his heart pounding with excitement. He knows *the fish will tire quickly. He peels the line back with his free hand, letting it coil in the water around him. As he steadily draws the line toward him he knows he has it. He has the fish. With the line still taut and stretched, it is finally in the water almost where he stands. He reaches down to pull the fish out.*

As he yanks it out of the water he screams in horror. There is no fish hooked to his line. It is the head of his dead aunt, her eyes open and yellow as if she is looking into his soul.

The Boy lurched upright from his pallet of straw. His tee shirt was again soaked with perspiration. For a moment, he couldn't breathe. He felt and could almost hear the rapid thumping of his heart within his thin, shallow chest. He looked about him. Nothing moved, no sound. Nothing. Finally, still breathing quick and shallow, he lay back down and this time fell into a fitful, dreamless sleep.

The sun rose over the distant tree line behind the barn and shot bright rays of light between the wall planks onto his face. He sat up, the dry straw softly crunching beneath him. He pulled his knees up to his chest and wrapped his arms around them. The terrible nightmare came to him in a shiver. Stupid, he thought, just stupid. Just unreasonable, unreachable. Not so much the decapitated aunt, but the trout fishing. Seeing himself there in the white-water fishing like the man on the cover of the magazine. Like he was *somebody.* He knew he would never be like that man. He was alone and doomed. There were no connections, being a part of something. To a place. But he had no place. He had seen only hopelessness and death. These were his connections now.

A vague new fear moved through him, not suddenly but stealthily, creeping into his body like a disease. He thought about the Deputy who was certainly looking for him. It was a miracle he hadn't been spotted on the highway last night. What they would do with him and where they would take him. A ward of the state, he had overheard a case worker say once to someone as he sat in the hard wooden chair against the green wall. He remembered the smells, septic and sour. And the two men. They are out there somewhere for sure.

As he pushed open the barn door he squinted in the bright morning sun. Maybe I should go back to the trailer and get my stuff. Some tee shirts, he thought as he pulled the front of the shirt he was wearing up to his nose. I stink. No, he couldn't go back there. They might be there waiting on him. Or the police nosing around. No, he'd get to the carnival. Russellville could not be far away now. Maybe an hour or two, and the carnival lot just a mile beyond that.

He made his way across the field, toward the road. As he approached the barbed wire fence he spotted blackberry vines clinging to several of the wobbly fence posts and the strands of wire. The vines sagged with huge, luscious pods of the dark ripe fruit. He knelt in the sedge beside one, pulled off a berry and popped it into his mouth. Then another and another. He ate the berries voraciously until his appetite was satiated. He was thirsty so he walked back of the shack and looked around, but could not find a well. Filled in, he guessed. He would have to wait for water.

CHAPTER 17

He reached Russellville sooner than he thought. Although it was a familiar place to him, now it did not seem so now. In his mind he had already removed himself from here, these kinds of people, from the pressing in on him. He hated it here. There was some traffic, mostly pickup trucks, and a school bus. As the bus slowly and noisily accelerated from the traffic light, he looked up to see the silhouetted heads of the children, some half dozing, as it passed by. A small boy looked down at him dully, his face blank and pallid pressed against a window fogged inside from his breathe. Then it seemed to just vanish in a cloud of black, oily diesel exhaust. He turned away and walked on.

He stopped at the café and gazed inside through the plate glass window, blotched and streaked with condensation. None of the few tables scattered in the dining area was occupied, but there were a few patrons sitting listlessly at the counter, bent over mugs of coffee. He massaged the bills in his pocket between his fingers. He wished he had not eaten the blackberries. His stomach felt hard and ached a little. He was not hungry.

He pulled open the door and stepped inside and was immediately engulfed in the almost icy air of the air-conditioned room. Coming in from the warm humid outside, it had surprised him and a quick shiver ran through his body. The cold air was heavy with the smell of stale grease and coffee. He took the counter stool nearest the entrance, away from the others. An aproned cook, his back to him, was frying bacon on the flat, black iron grill behind the counter. He then gathered the strips of meat with a large fork and held them above the surface of the grill, letting the grease drain from them, splattering and popping, onto the hot black steel. He placed the bacon on a plate with a mound of eggs, scrambled hard, and slid it haphazardly down the counter to a man sitting there. He wiped his hands on the apron and stepped back up to where the Boy was sitting.

"What'll you have, sonny boy?" asked the cook, his sweaty face close.

"Can I have a drink of water?"

"Just water? You don't want nothing to eat?"

"Just a glass of water. That's all. I'll pay for it."

"Well, I ain't goin' to charge you for water. You want ice in it, I reckon."

"No, just water."

The man in the apron took a plastic glass from a shelve above the grill, filled it with water, and placed it on the counter before the Boy.

"Thanks," said the Boy as he drank from the glass, never taking his eyes off the man. After he had drained the glass, he slid off the stool and made his way to the door. The cook eyed him as he exited and shrugged as he pushed open the door and vanished into the street.

None of the people in the cars and trucks whizzing by him seemed oblivious to him as he strode along the road toward the field where he had seen the carnival, in the Preacher's field. He too was unaware of them. He felt invisible and almost as if he was floating along toward his destination and perhaps, he hoped, what would be his destiny. His way out.

Walking eastward, the road curved slightly to his left. The sun was well up, already nothing but a white glare in his face. But it was still early. As the road straightened from the curve, he stopped and shaded his eyes with the palm of his hand. And there it was, beyond him, no more than a quarter of a mile. From here it was vague and shadowy, and he couldn't make out much, but that was all right. Spread over the Preacher's field. Like his heart, his pace quickened.

He stood silently and still in front of the entrance peering at the incongruous assembly of small, mostly wooden, structures. They were painted, all different colors. Like a rainbow, it occurred to him. But a dingy, faded-colored rainbow. It was like a three-dimensional, dull and faded photograph. The glassless windows of the roofed cubicles and booths were either shuttered or covered with canvas tarps tied down tightly with rope run through grommets along the edges. Nothing looked permanent. There were no foundations. They just sat squarely on the level ground. It was as if someone at any moment might come and tear them down, or apart, and take them away. Or a storm might sweep them into oblivion. Signs on top of each structure gave its purpose: *Cotton Candy, Corn Dogs, Chili Dogs with Fries, Caps, Pinwheels*, and more. Nothing moved inside. There was no sign of life. This was the front end of the carnival.

On either side of the ten-yard wide space, just beyond where he stood, were two kiosks with openings facing the road. One was painted a gaudy yellow trimmed in purple and the other blue and red. Under the window of each hung a worn but neatly printed sign: *Tickets*. They flanked the open space like two empty sockets from which the eyes had been gouged. The two ticket booths were connected with a heavy, low-slung rusty chain, blocking off the entrance to the carnival.

He stepped over the chain and stood in the carnival yard. Almost exactly where the Preacher's big plywood sign had been planted. He looked over the ground to find the post holes but they weren't there. He could see from here that aisles, wide walkways in the dirt, radiated out from the vending stands. The widest one seemed to cut through the heart of the carnival like an open wound and he could see the Ferris wheel beyond. It stood silently like a huge steel spider web. Not far from it he could see the Bullet with its steel erector-set arm perpendicular to the ground, with one of the enclosed gondolas held skyward at one end. The other low, near the ground.

At first disappointed with the stark shabbiness of the carnival as it unveiled itself in the scowl of the morning sun, it then suddenly occurred to him that he was finally in another world. When he had stepped across the chain ostensibly blocking the entrance, he had moved quickly and inexplicably from the hostile terrifying world that he had always known into a strange mystical universe where the old rules might not apply. Where it had seemed improbable to him before, now survival seemed possible, maybe even likely.

He strode slowly down the wide open aisle toward the big rides at the back. What the carnies called the *back end.* Stands and booths, all shut up or empty lined the way on either side. The walkway intersected with another one at what seemed to him to be the very center of the carnival. Down the way to his right there were large tents with low stages, or platforms, in front. One of the signs at the intersection, staked into the ground, had an arrow and read: *Girls! Girls! Girls!* He wasn't sure what it meant or what there was to be found down the path.

The aisle to his left was also lined with stands and cubicles. There was also a sign with an arrow. *Side-Show: Freaks-This Way!* He hesitated, but then continued his slow trek down the way he had started, toward the back end.

He did not see anyone nor heard any voices as he walked. The silence was eerie and pervasive, but it did not frighten him. He had known fear and this was not it. He knew there were people here. Somewhere. He finally came to a large open expanse where all the big rides waited, still, paralyzed as if frozen in time. He glanced over at the Ferris wheel to his left. He had not imagined it would stand so high, its chipped angle iron frame baking in the sun. To the other side of the yard was the Bullet.

Then out across the open area beyond, he saw something. They were scattered about in haphazard rows, some seemed as randomly placed as stars. The sun glinted off their metallic surfaces. He recognized them and knew what they were. They were like the Preacher's. Trailers and campers. A few were painted and faded but most were just bare aluminum, all dented to varying degrees. This is where the carnival people live, he said to himself. They are asleep. This is the way they live. Moving from place to place. Not staying anywhere too long. They don't need the world, or schools, or foster homes. They are connected with themselves and to each other. To the carnival. This is where I'll live too.

Without really thinking about it, he instinctively made his way across the narrow expanse of the dusty field to where the trailers were. It was as if he were being drawn there. As he approached this ragged, odd conglomeration of wheeled dwellings he heard a loud report, almost like a gun shot. He whirled back to his left from where the sound had come and saw a man clad only in undershorts strolling to a nearby trailer. He had just exited a portable toilet and the 'shot' and been the spring-loaded door slamming shut behind him. He had not seen the Boy. He swallowed hard and called out.

"Hey, Mister!"

Surprised at the voice, the man turned to him as he approached.

"What the hell you doing back here? Scared the shit out of me."

"You the boss man?"

"Hell, no, I ain't no boss man. You go on and get the hell out of here. Damn townies!" The man turned away and reached for the door knob.

"I want a job. A job with the carnival."

"Look, kid, forget it. Every damn town we set up in there's always some kid comes and wants to join the carnival. Except most of them at least show up in the evening when we're open. You best get on out of here while the gettin's good."

"Does the boss man stay back here, too?"

"Of course, he does. Where the hell you think he stays, in the nearby Waldorf Astoria?" The man laughed. The Boy didn't understand the joke.

"I need to talk to him, that's all."

"Like I said, forget it. It ain't going to happen. Not out here in the dirt and sun. Dammit it, it's already hot as hell. Look, kid, lot of these boys, the carnies I mean, ain't as nice as me and would as soon beat the shit out of you as not. You go waking them up at this time of day and that's exactly what'll happen. You best get on out of here. Go on back home. Your mama will be wondering where you are."

The Boy stood there as the man entered the trailer, but then he stopped in the doorway and looked back at the him.

"Come back tonight. Not here on the back lot, but to the carnival. Have a little fun. Spend all your money. If you got any, that is."

"I got money," The Boy replied quietly as the trailer door slammed shut, and then he walked away.

CHAPTER 18

With the camp fire dying behind him he made his way to the parked police cruiser. The headlights had been left on and he could see them through the trees and undergrowth. As he drew closer he could hear the deep, throaty hum of the engine which had also been left running. Once to the car, he slipped in under the wheel. There was chatter on the radio.

"Car two, what's your ten-twenty? Come in, car two." Then static. Then again, "Car 2, please report. What is your ten-twenty? Car two, do you read me?" Over and over again.

He then grabbed a fist full of wires leading from the radio to under the dashboard and yanked them. Hard. The radio fell silent.

He made a U-turn in the dirt road and drove back toward the creek, looking for the Boy. He used the spotlight that was mounted on the door post and combed the dark woods with it. Here and there the green eyes of a deer stared back at him, or some other creature, but there was no Boy. Finally, he gave up and turned around and headed back to the county highway, but driving slow, piercing the forest around him with the spotlight.

On a hunch, he drove to River Road and stopped on the ridge above the blue trailer. He could hardly see its hunched and beaten form in the scant moon light, but all was blackness between it and the river. Lifeless. He finally pulled back onto the county road and drove casually toward Russellville.

The Boy may have fled the woods and the creek and be on the highway, walking, but he had seen nothing. In the darkness he had not seen the deserted shack and small barn beyond the barbed wire fence that ran along the road when he had driven past it. If he had, he would have thought nothing of it anyway. Like a mindless, hungry predator he drove on. He'd drive the police car a few more miles, just to get him down the road a little more toward Troy, but he knew he'd have to abandon it soon. Then he'd find that little bastard.

He passed through Russellville and then by the carnival. It suddenly struck him. There was something about the carnival that excited him and made him feel uneasy and nervous. The people. The children. Yeah, all them kids, he thought. All of 'em in there eatin' cotton candy, ridin' the rides, jis' walkin' around. The Boy was nothin' but a kid. If he could, he'd be at the carnival. I'll look for him there. Bet that's where he'd wind up. In time. Jis' maybe.

After passing by the carnival lot he began to look for a place to ditch the car. He figured he was already on borrowed time, but it didn't matter. Not now. He couldn't get the carnival, or the Boy, off his mind. Slumped low in the seat, he had glanced over at the brightly lit carnival as he drove by. Cars had filled the open field next to it and were parked along the shoulder of the road on both sides. People seemed to be everywhere. Coming and going. Loitering around the ticket booths at the entrance. He could hear the muted music of the carousel through the open window. He drove on.

The trees and bush hugged close to both sides of the road just beyond narrow ditches. Up ahead the headlights reflected off a bent, rusting *No Trespassing* sign nailed to a tree just off the road on the left. He stopped the car in the middle of the highway and looked at the sign. There seemed to be some kind of trail leading off down into the woods. But it was hard to tell in the darkness and the overgrowth. He brightened the headlights and then turned slowly from the road and into the dense growth of weeds, kudzu, and gnarled, scrubby water oaks. Finally, well away from the highway, deep in the woods, the trail abruptly ended. It seemed late and he was tired. He cut the engine, then crawled into the back seat and almost instantly was asleep.

There was a noise and he immediately sat upright, still in the back seat of the car. He waited and listened, but heard nothing more. Probably jis' a squirrel or raccoon, he thought. He wondered what time it was. No way to tell deep in the wood like this. Then he thought of the Boy and the carnival. Might still be open, he reasoned. Maybe it wasn't that late after all. But the Boy couldn't be there. Not yet.

He then got out of the car and walked cautiously back up the trail he had driven down, always keeping to the edge of it. He finally came to the highway. He could see the carnival lights in the distance, down the road toward Russellville. A car whizzed by, blowing the horn. He crossed the road where there was a deep gully that ran parallel to it. Almost crouching, he made his way toward the lights.

He stood for a while to the side, in the shadows near the ticket booths and watched. People milled around outside and there were those entering and leaving the carnival. Eventually he made his way around to where the cars were parked, some up close facing the rear of the stalls. It was dark back there except for narrow slants of yellow light from inside the carnival. There was no fence. Well away from the front entrance, he slipped between a popcorn wagon and a game booth, and stepped unnoticed into the crowd of people. Unshaven and grubby, he could have easily been taken for a carnie.

He strolled along the edge of the slow moving river of people like an apparition, barely visible, looking irrationally for the Boy. Once he spat and grinned when he had seen a boy up ahead in the throng with his back to him. As he approached, he saw that it was not the Boy when he turned to face him, then walked away with his friends. He knew the Boy would be alone. But he was here or *would* be. Somewhere near. He could feel it.

The food stalls and games kiosks began to close down. A knot of men still lingered around the outside stage of the girlie show, but the crowd was thinning out quickly. He made his way to near the entrance. He leaned indifferently against a power pole, watching people exit the carnival. But his intent was anything *but* indifferent. A group of young men approached, laughing and cursing, walking unsteadily toward the exit. One of them drained the contents of pint bottle and then tossed it to the ground. It skidded across the dirt near to where he stood. The drunk young man looked at him, squinting as if he wasn't sure what he was seeing or maybe wondering if there really was anyone there at all. He stared back at him and fingered the hawk bill knife in his pocket. The young man's friends said something he couldn't hear, and they all laughed. Then they moved on through the gate and vanished into the night.

The carnival was now deserted except for a few tired carnies tying things down, securing locks, kicking trash aside. Then they soon trudged to the back lot. With only a few of the pole lights left on, the place was bathed in an eerie and garish yellow bleakness, more a fog than light.

Maybe the young'un hadn't had time to make it this far, he thought. He reminded himself that he had driven here. The Boy was afoot so he must be on the road somewhere. He'd just missed him, that's all. He'll be along. Don't make no difference anyhow. I'll git him.

The Big man slipped out the exit and made his way along the highway in the darkness, back to the Deputy's car, tripping over roots, brushing tree limbs from his face, and cursing. Scratched and bleeding, he crawled into the back seat. I'll go back there tomorrow night, I reckon, and he'll be there. For damn sure, he'll be there. He then fell into a deep, coma-like sleep.

CHAPTER 19

It was a well past noon when he trudged back to the café. He sat at the counter where he had before and ordered a grilled cheese sandwich with a glass of water. The cook flipped the greasy sandwich from the grill onto a small plate and placed it on the counter in front of him. He looked down at it for a moment and then up at the big round clock facing him from the wall where the bored and sweaty cook now leaned, smoking a cigarette. He glanced down at the sandwich again and at the melted orange cheese oozing from it and gelling on the plate. He wasn't as hungry as he had thought, but he lifted the heavy sandwich to his mouth and began munching it. He ate most of it, leaving some of the saturated crust stuck to the plate. He looked up at the clock again. It seemed the hands had hardly moved at all.

"Do you know what time the carnival opens?" he asked the cook who had turned back to the grill and was pressing already thin hamburger patties flat on it with a spatula. Either the cook didn't hear him or maybe he just ignored the question. He didn't respond.

"I reckon the rides open up at four o'clock," offered the man, obese and grizzled, sitting at the counter a couple of stools down drinking coffee. "But the good stuff don't start 'til after dark. No matter none, they won't let no young'un in the side shows anyhow." His laugh was hoarse and lewd. The Boy looked at him and said nothing.

He sipped the water from the plastic glass and stared at the reluctant clock. He finally left the café and walked back toward the carnival lot. As he approached, he saw that the heavy chain was still stretched across the entrance. He sat down in the shade of one of the ticket booths, his back to it. He pulled his knees up to his chest and rested his head on them and waited.

He was awakened from a shallow doze when he heard someone fidgeting with the chain where one end of it was padlocked to a low steel post. He sat up instantly. The man had disengaged the end of the chain from the post and was dragging it across the ground toward him. He wore tattered leather gloves, but was he was freshly shaven. He was square and heavy-set, but not fat. The Boy noted the clean shirt tucked neatly into his trousers. As the man approached, he quickly stood up and brushed himself off.

"Is the carnival open now?"

The man had not seen the Boy and was startled, but only for an instant.

"What you doing out here, kid?" the man asked gruffly.

"Waiting for the carnival to open, that's all."

"Nothing wrong with that, I guess. Getting ready to open up the rides and some of the concession stands," said the man as he coiled the chain around the post.

"Is the boss here?" asked the Boy, his voice rising, excitement mixed with impatience.

"Why you want to know that for?"

"I need to talk to him, that all. That's what I come for. To talk to the boss of the carnival."

"Well, young man, looks like it might be your lucky day. They don't call me boss, at least not to my face, but I'm the owner of this here show. What can I do for you?"

The Boy sighed deeply and looked down at his shoes in the dirt. Strangely, he felt a great feeling of relief come over him. His fists which had been clenched tightly at his side loosened and relaxed. He looked up at the man.

"I want a job. I mean, I need a job. I want to be with the carnival. I want to be a part of it. That's why I been here waitin' here. I want to be part of it. I can work."

"Whoa, now, son! Every kid I run into wants to join the carnival or the circus or whatever. This ain't no place for a kid like you. Your folks know you come out here?"

"I ain't got no folks."

"Well, sorry, but I can't help you. We're not hiring any townies at this stop. You best run along now."

"But I can work. I want to work. I don't take no lookin' after."

The man chuckled and thrust his hands into his trouser pockets.

"No, I expect you don't. But we ain't picking up kids at every hole-in-the wall town neither. I got enough trouble from the cops as it is. Don't need no snotty-nose kid wanting to be a carnie."

"Yeah, that's it! I want to be a carnie!"

"Look, young fella, I got things to see about, but tell you what I'll do. See all this trash and paper scattered all over the ground?"

"I see it."

"You work for a couple of hours picking up liter here around the lot and I'll pay you five dollars. And I'll let you in the carnival for free. How's that for a deal?"

The Boy thought for a moment.

"Can I work tomorrow too? I mean pickin' up the trash."

"Seems like you *do* want to work, but I can't help you. See, the show will be pulling up and moving on once we close down this evening."

"The carnival's already movin'? You just got here. I know because I know what was here before you came."

"We don't stay anywhere long. A week at most. Little ole town like this one here can't support a show but a night or two."

The man's word excited the Boy. What he said about moving on, not staying anyplace for very long. The carnival was its own world. The people in it, the carnies, were a part of it. They were connected to it and to each other. They didn't need anybody else. Or anything. Connected to it just like it was a family. They just *had* to let him in.

"Where you takin' the carnival?" asked the Boy.

"Leaving here for sure. Macon maybe. Then on down to South Georgia, Valdosta, and then to Florida for the winter. You see, son, it's a hard life. Not one for a kid like you."

It was a perfect life. Moving, faceless, but connected in a way. It was perfect.

"I'll pick up trash for you, mister."

"Atta Boy. See that fella over there?" the man pointed to a man beyond the gate, inside the carnival lot. He held a spear-like shaft and was jabbing it into the pieces of scattered paper, cups, and other litter scattered on the ground, and then peeling it off into a steel, open-top barrel.

"Yeah, I see can see him."

"That's my main cleanup man. Just go on over there and tell him I hired you for the afternoon. He'll cuss and grumble because he don't like townies, but he'll put you to work. I'll come find you after while and we'll settle up."

"All right," replied the Boy.

He shook his head and walked away from the Boy, back to the office trailer in the back lot. Townies, he thought, can't live with 'em, can't live without 'em. He'd had his share of problems with them. Mostly fights on the carnival grounds. Or a drunk crawling up on the stage of one of the strip shows thinking that he was suddenly in love. Police always blamed him or one of the carnies. He couldn't help the fact that the carnival always seemed to attract some of the town's worse reprobates. Mostly just good ole boys looking for a good time, a reprise from their dull, dead-end lives. Get drunk, go to the carnival, raise a little hell. No harm in that.

There seemed to always be a kid or two who thought they wanted to join the carnival. They'd come slinking around the office trailer looking for him. Sometimes they even brought a suitcase or backpack with them. Their old man beat them, or they'd been kicked out of school, or had knocked up little Suzy next door. He'd heard and seen it all. He rarely gave them the time of day. Told one or two to go home and think about, and then come back to see him. He couldn't remember one who ever did. Come back, that is.

The kid this afternoon struck him somehow as different from the others. He couldn't put his finger on it. Something in his face, his eyes. It was like a kind of desperate determination, or something. It wasn't clear to him. The part about his having no folks sounded a little strange, but had a ring of truth to it, the way the Boy had said it and had looked him straight in the eyes when he did. It had a finality to it. Or might have. And his staying around to work picking up trash. Like he *really* was alone. This wasn't likely though, and the owner knew it. His instincts told him it spelled trouble. Just the kind he didn't need.

Especially after the last time, in North Carolina, up near Gastonia.

One of the strippers, Kandy Kane she called herself, was crazy. He had known it, but she did damn good work, always packed the house. Her act was wild and crazy too, way over the top with what the law usually allowed, but he had somehow avoided trouble. So far. But Kandy had a penchant for young boys, fifteen or sixteen, and maybe young girls too, but he'd been able to keep an eye on her so nothing serious had occurred. Then after a show one night the folks of a kid came looking for him. It was late and the carnival had closed down for the night. But they brought the police with them. They were pushy and bullied everybody, the owner and a few workers who were standing around. They started to come down hard on one of the barkers. It turned out he had worked the strip show that night. When a big, particularly nasty cop threatened to take him in, he mentioned that he had seen a boy of that description earlier. When the policeman grabbed him by the collar, he said that the boy might with Kandy. Well, he was. Kandy was arrested on the spot and the carnival was given to dawn to clear out of town, which it did. Such was life with the carnival.

The lights of the carnival glowed brightly as a hot dusk crept in from the eastern sky. The cleanup man *had* grumbled and cussed, but he had spent the late afternoon walking the lot, picking up the litter tossed aside by the townies and carnies the night before. For a few hours at least, it was like he had actually been a carnie. At least that's the way he felt. He reached into the pocket of his jeans and felt the crispness of the folded five-dollar bill.

By now all the concessions stands, the games, the rides, and the side shows were open. The carnival *did* look different at night. Everything seemed to glitter. It all seemed new somehow. There were people everywhere—some just strolling the aisles, looking for ways to spend their money. The usual dead, dry smell of the baked earth was, for a while, overcome by the aromas of French fries and over-cooked corn dogs mixed with the sugary smells of cotton candy. The people smiled as if they were having a good time, as if they were excited about it all. The hawkers and barkers tried to sound enthusiastic, and maybe they were. To them the townies were either flatties—no face at all—or marks. Not real people, just suckers. Easy money any way you looked at it.

He stopped across from an open booth and watched a man, a thin emaciated woman at his shoulder, throw balls at a stack of solid steel objects shaped like milk bottles. He threw hard and knocked down a few, but never enough to win one of the pastel stuffed animals that hung on a peg board beside the man working the game who occasionally glanced down at his wrist watch. After tossing the last ball, which missed the steel milk bottles altogether, the man laughed loudly and walked away, pulling the scrawny women with him. The Boy moved on.

He finally came an intersection that he recognized from earlier that morning. He looked down to his right and saw a large crowd, mostly men, bunched up in front of a tent. A man, a barker, paced back and forth on the low stage in front of the men. As he paced, he spoke into the microphone that he held in a sweaty hand. It is like one of those preachers I've seen on TV, thought the Boy, on Sunday morning. A Sunday somewhere, some place, long ago. It was like he was preaching. Pacing, sweating and preaching. The Boy could not make out what the barker was saying to the crowd but he figured he wasn't preaching. Not church-preaching anyhow.

He turned down the wide aisle. He was curious to know what the crowd of men found so interesting and to know what the barker was saying to them. But before he had gone very far he looked up and caught the eye of someone he recognized.

"Where the hell you think you going, young fella?" the man looked down at him, grinning. It was the owner.

"Nowhere. I'm just walkin' around lookin' at things. That's all. Just lookin'."

"Well, that's fine and dandy but you ain't going down there."

"Why not? I ain't hurtin' nothing."

"Because I said you ain't, that's why. I guess you know what that is down there? What all them crackers are gawking at?"

"The sign says 'Girls'."

"That's right. They ain't exactly girls. Not like what you might be used to seeing."

The girl in the cut-off jean and tee shirt flashed into the Boy's mind. The girl standing up on the bank looking down at him and not smiling. The girl with the two men. She was what he was used to seeing.

"I'll just walk on past there. Can't hurt nothing."

"Yeah, and might just get interested. There's likely a cop or two wandering around the lot. They see I let a kid near a girly show they'll close me down. Not that that would be a great loss in this burg." The owner put his hands on the Boy's shoulder and turned him back up the aisle. "Go get you some cotton candy and ride the rides. That's what normal kids do."

Normal kids, he thought as he walked away. I don't know what that is, but it sure ain't me. He knew the Deputy would be out looking for him. He'd find him and he'd end up in another home with some haggard old woman getting a check every month for feeding him and sending him to school. Her husband or boyfriend, if she had one, would be a drunk or dope-head and slap him around. He sighed deeply and sauntered slump-shouldered toward the Ferris wheel. I figured that stupid Deputy would've found me by now, he said to himself. He will, I reckon, and there ain't nothing I can do about it.

As he made his way leisurely through the throng of people he began to notice them more closely, individually. He looked into the faces of the young ones. Young, like he was. Smiling or giggling, enthralled by the excitement and lights and sounds of the carnival around them. They all seemed to him foolishly happy. For a moment, in his envy, he hated them. Stupid redneck punks, he thought. Just like me. But he was on the outside looking in to a world he didn't know or would ever know. Crackers, the owner had called them. Peeing in their pants over an old broken down and grimy carnival come to town. Blowing what little money they had on junk and French-fried smelling dreams. Maybe he was lucky to be on his own, alone. It felt better this way. He'd get to the foster home, he knew that, and be just as alone and unconnected. But damn if some drunk, slobbering old man would beat him this time. By now he was thinking killing someone wouldn't be that hard to do. To protect yourself.

He caught the eye of a girl, young as he was maybe. She smiled sheepishly, trying not to reveal her braces. He looked hard into her face as he stopped walking. She quickly looked away and melted into the slow flow of the crowd as it passed by him. He stood there and watched her disappear, as an odd and curious feeling, almost a shiver, engulfed him briefly but then vanished just as quickly. Was that what connection felt like, he wondered, and then dismissed it as just chance, like an accident. Just something random. Maybe it never even happened. There was no beckoning, no connection to the strange inexplicable lure he felt within himself. Not the stirring. Not at all like the feeling and memory that he had cultivated of the girl at the creek that day. She had exerted a power over him in a way he could not understand. It had not been a pleasant thing—the vile men with her, the whiskey-laced cursing. But for a moment, just for an instant, he could forget all that and just see her alone, staring down at him standing in the creek no longer laughing, but with something else in her eyes. It became a pleasant thing to him. He could not forget it.

At the central intersection of the walkways he turned right, into the mass of people moving toward the big rides.

CHAPTER 20

Though deep in the woods and blocked from the direct, hot penetrating rays of the sun, the interior of the patrol car became an oven in the oppressive heat of late morning. The air was heavy and motionless. It had woken him, his face lying in its own drool and the sweaty flesh sticking to the vinyl-covered back seat where he slept. He crawled out of the car, almost stumbling to the ground, and made his way deeper into the overgrowth beyond the vehicle. He knew he had already taken a great risk by sleeping in the Deputy's car, but fatigue and desperation had overcome his instincts. They'd find it soon enough, but he'd be gone. Couldn't pin it on him anyway. Nobody knew his face but the Boy and I'm bettin' he'll show up at that carnival, he thought. Beyond that, he had no thoughts.

By noon he had finished off what remained of the canned food he had taken from the dead woman's trailer. The Small man crossed his mind and he cursed him aloud in a low, fetid breath. Let that po-lice scare him to death. Run like a rabbit. Probably layin' up drunk with some of his kin up in Munro County by now. Hope he got snake bit runnin' through them woods at night. Copperheads and timber rattlers would've been out crawling around. For a few moments the Big man indulged himself with a vivid picture in his mind of his ragged accomplice lying on the ground in the darkness groaning, his leg aching and swollen, the skin turning scarlet, then black, as the venom spread from the two deep fang marks on his calf. He'd be suckin' wind by now, tryin' to breathe. Probably done throwed up all over hisself, about blind too. The Big man chuckled aloud.

He tossed the empty cans into the bush, relieved himself, and sat dozing against a diseased water oak. He'd rest a spell. Wait until near dark and walk back down the road to the carnival. The Boy'd be there. Take care of this here business and move on.

It was mid-afternoon when he woke suddenly. He did not move. Through the trees and brush to his right he heard the rustle of dry leaves. Squirrels maybe. Then voices. The sounds were coming from the direction of the abandoned patrol car. They had found it. They were close, but he could not see them, nor they him. He eased himself up slowly, his back pressed against the trunk of the tree. Once erect he rubbed a palm over the pocket of his pants and felt the reassuring bulk of the hawk bill through the filthy fabric. He moved slowly away from the tree and away from the source of the sounds. He planted each foot silently, almost softly, in front of the other and made his way quickly into the thick woods beyond.

He would go deeper into the forest and wait. Then near dusk, but while there was still some light, he would circle back to the highway, away from where he had driven the car into the brush and left it. This should bring him very near the carnival lot. He was not too worried about the local police now. With the patrol car discovered, they would be too busy and excited to notice or be concerned about some drifter at a carnival. Even if he was seen they would likely assume he was just another carnie, grimy and down on his luck.

Deep in the woods, he rested, snoozing against a tree. It was dusk when he roused himself and started back toward the highway, circling away from where he had left the cruiser. It was hot and the underbrush was thick. He sweated and cursed as the briars tore at his bare arms and face.

Just after dark he arrived at the highway. He remained at the edge of the woods, but he could hear the sounds of carnival and see its yellow glow through the trees just beyond him across the road. Then slightly hunched over, he left the cover of the dark forest like a grisly, almost shapeless phantom escaping from its lair, crossed the highway and onto the carnival lot. He worked his way among the parked cars of the townies, searching for the opening between the backs of the stalls where he had entered the carnival grounds the night before. Finally, in the shadows ahead he spotted the low shaft of light. There was the opening. He kept low between the vehicles and slipped through the narrow opening. The parade of people, all faceless to him, was much larger than the night before. Don't matter none, he thought. I'll still find him. He strode across the bare dusty ground and melted into the throng, becoming a part of it.

CHAPTER 21

At the stand across from the Ferris wheel, he bought cotton candy and stood watching the operator, bored and impatient, load people into the gondolas. He would then pull the clutch handle causing the huge wheel to begin rotating slowly, picking up speed with each rotation. The Boy counted. The operator let the wheel rotate ten times before pulling the brake lever to slow it down, and then to stop it. The ride was over. Then it started over again. Load the people. Start the wheel. Ten rotations. Stop the wheel. Something about the precise regularity he liked. It became predictable. No wonder the operator was bored.

He soon became bored too. He turned his attention away from the Ferris wheel and began to watch the people strolling past him more closely. He figured if he stayed here, in one spot, the Deputy would eventually find him. He had resigned himself to it. Somehow, for a while, just being here in the crowd made things seem not so empty. But he *had* become empty. Empty inside as the hope of escaping faded and died like a snuffed-out candle flame. Stark, cold emptiness. He was without a name or a place or a future. He was alone.

Through the crowd ahead of him the Big man saw a Boy leaning against a light post, a cloud of pale blue cotton candy on a cardboard tube in his hand. His back to him, just there watching the people float by. He moved to the edge of the throng and slowly made his way to where the Boy was. He eased noiselessly up behind him and placed a squalid claw of a hand on the thin, unsuspecting shoulder. Startled, the Boy turned to look into the dead eyes of the gnarled face. The sickening stench of the breath from the face filled his nostrils. He suddenly shoved the thick web of cotton candy into the Big man's face and fled into the plodding and mindless crowd.

The man grinned as he wiped away the sugary mess from his face. He did not chase after the Boy, but followed him, walking swiftly, weaving between the townies. Brushing against some of them. Hearing them curse him, but not caring. Stalking him as if the Boy was a wounded animal. He watched as the Boy disappeared behind a dull, silver trailer, some carnie's home. They were in the back lot. He then edged silently along the opposite side of the trailer. He could hear the Boy's rapid breathing as he pressed himself against the back metallic wall. A stupid and malicious smile came to the man's thin lips. He sprang from the darkness and grabbed the Boy, keeping him pinned to the trailer.

"I gotchee now, you little bastard."

As the man, with one hand, fumbled in his pocket for the hawk bill the Boy managed to pull away from his grasp. He ran, almost stumbling, toward the lights and people of the midway. The man sprang after him grabbed him by his arm, pushing him against a light post. With the hot blood of an animal prepared to kill its prey, he seemed to be oblivious to the fact that he stood in a pool of pale yellow light and could be seen by anyone passing though there were not many people this far back in the lot.

"They know who you are," said the frightened Boy straining against the Big man's grip, his breath rapid and shallow. "There's a deputy sheriff looking for me right now, close by. Probably right here in the carnival."

"You mean that ole boy who was lookin' for ye up in

them woods near the creek?"

"He's looking for me now. He knows me. He's around here. Let me go!"

"I wouldn't worry myself none about that fat ole deputy. I opened him up like a ripe watermelon. He didn't make a sound, jis' looked surprised, standing there trying to hold his guts inside him. Naw, I don't reckon he can help you none now," he said with a coarse chuckle.

The Boy struggled and attempted to cry for help as the man place his hand over his mouth, pulling him out of the light. He had the knife opened in his other hand. The Boy, all but helpless against this hulking, mindless predator, did not stop struggling. Then he saw something over the shoulder behind his assailant. Someone, a shadow, stepped into the dim light.

"What the hell's going on here?" asked the shadow.

The Big man froze, but did not release his grip on the Boy.

"None of your concern. Jis' this here young'un of mine don't know how to act. Jis' about to give him a whoopin', that's all. You best be movin' on and mind ye own business." The Big man kept his stare focused on the Boy and did not turn around to the shadow as he spoke.

"Well, I'm making it my business. Let the Boy go and I mean right now."

The man, still clutching the Boy, turned toward the voice, his ugly mouth in a snarl.

"Like I said, mister, ye best be movin' on." He gripped the hawk bill and held it tightly against his leg with his free hand. The shadow did not move.

"I been watching you since you snuck in here. I've been dealing with townies, hicks like you, all my life. I own this show and I'll tell you one last time to release the Boy."

"Well, I might jis' have to settle with you first, Mr. Owner," he said, easing his hold on the Boy.

The owner was wearing a thin jacket which seemed inexplicable in the night heat. Then the Boy saw him push back the flap of it. His hand moved to his belt and there was suddenly something in his hand. Then a distinct metallic click.

"Anytime you feel froggy, redneck, you just leap," said the owner, the revolver dangling at his side." The Big man released the Boy and turned toward the owner in the murky light. "I don't know what this is all about, but I'm not having this kind of trouble on my lot. This man your daddy?" He looked down at the Boy.

"No, he ain't my daddy. Ain't no kin of mine. I ain't got no kin."

"You get the hell out of here and off this lot," said the owner to the Big man.

Still gripping the hawk bill, he glared at the owner but did not move. For a tense moment, no one in the circle of light moved. The he expertly closed the knife with one hand and slipped it into his pocket. He turned back to the Boy.

"Okay, boy, for now. But I'll be out there a waitin' on ye. Ye can be sure of that." He chuckled angrily and sauntered off toward the midway.

The owner watched him as he disappeared into the distant crowd of townies. He turned to the Boy.

"You all right?"

"Yeah, I'm all right."

"Look, I can't afford to get messed up with you locals. I got enough problems with the police as it is. I'm going to go follow that piece of shit and make sure he's off the lot. You can wait here a while, but you need to go home. You can't stay here."

Go home, the Boy thought. He almost laughed out loud. Go home. What a joke.

"All right."

"Go on over to a concession stand and get yourself a soda. You got any money left?"

"Yeah, I got some."

The owner shook his head slightly and then turned back toward the midway. The Boy watched him disappear into the crowd.

Fear rose again in the Boy, but it did not debilitate him. He had lived with it for days now and it had become almost a part of him. He had to admit to himself that he had felt some relief when he had resigned himself to being placed back in a foster home. That's why he had decided to just wait for the Deputy to show up and take him away. But there would be no deputy. He knew that now. Always before, there had seemed to be a way out, some trick or manipulation or just to wait, something. But not this time. I just got to think, he said to himself, just got to figure it out.

As long as he was on the carnival lot he would be safe, he knew that. But the carnival is leaving tonight, the owner had told him. In a few short hours it would dissolve into the night and the lot would stand empty and desolate. It would be like the carnival and the Preacher had never existed, both unreal things. But he knew the man would be waiting for him, hiding in a gully or in the brush along the highway, some place
dark from which there would be no escape. Some place where he would die.

He wandered back into the lights and among the people who moved languidly and faceless around him. But he did not see them now nor they him. He walked slowly back to where he had watched the Ferris wheel. For the first time he felt the weight of fatigue sweep over him and pull down on him like bags of wet sand tied to his body. He was tired. He was tired of this night, of these stupid people shuffling past him. He was tired of running, of being afraid. But mostly he was tired of pretending that he was somebody when he knew that he wasn't.

Now it seemed to him that the people just floated past him like mindless apparitions. There were no laughing children, no couples holding hands with anticipation, no pretty young girls smiling sweetly at him. He was aware of no sounds. Nothing was in focus, nothing distinct. He came to the carousel and watched as the once colorful, bassword-carved horses whose paint was now chipped and faded revolved eerily in a joyless infinite journey. No one was riding. It was growing late. The children had all gone home. As he stood there, seemingly almost hypnotized by the movement of the ride, he felt the futility and senselessness of it—round and round and round, never reaching the end. It was as if he were outside himself, looking down on it all, including himself entranced by the carousel. But he could not hear the music. There must have been music. But he could not hear it. Maybe it is, he thought, hopeless after all.

Finally, he moved away from the sadness of the carousel and continued back toward the Ferris wheel. The crowds had thinned and were much sparser now. The people, their money spent on a few hours of self-induced make-believe, were disappearing into the hot night. Townies, the owner had called them. Called him a townie, too, but he wasn't one. How he wished now that he were.

Strangely, once back gazing at the Ferris wheel, away from the people, he felt better. *I can figure this out. I'm smart, smarter than that smelly big man. Not so strong maybe, but smart. Smarter than him.* He suddenly remembered the lot, this same lot, where he had been with the Preacher only days before. Beyond, from where the carnival was now, was a high tree line, deep thick woods. He might could sneak through the back lot where the trailers and trucks were parked and make it to the woods. *Surely I can do that,* he reasoned. *And then what? Keep running, I reckon.*

He pushed his way through the thinning crowd, looking back every few moments to see if the owner was back there, still following him out. He was. Like a predator knowing where its wounded prey lies helpless and waiting, he had to fight his instincts to double back and find the Boy. The owner could identify him now, but it did not seem to matter to him. Somehow he would do it, and then run, escape. It wasn't a matter of if, but rather when and where. Damn the owner.

He finally reached the front of the carnival and shuffled out with the other people. It was late and he knew the carnival would shut down soon. He crossed the highway, jumped over a ditch and stood for a while at the edge of the bushes and low, gnarled trees, watching the carnival entrance across the way. Then he squatted beside a tree and waited.

It's midnight and the last ride—the Ferris wheel—shuts down. The bored and weary operator opens the bar of the gondola to release the last of the occupants. Two giggling teenagers stand up unsteadily and exit, nearly stumbling down the low, short ramp. One passes the joint to the other, but no one notices or cares. Carnies with wrenches seem to appear from nowhere and begin to disassemble the wheel. Most of the sideshows and game booths are already down and are being loaded onto the trucks and trailers. A generator hums dully somewhere on the back lot, keeping the low, pole-mounted lights glaring eerily as the workers silently and sullenly go about their tasks. Some of the hawkers, who are not really carnies, are already in trailers with the strippers.

As night begins to give way to a gray and drizzling dawn, the carnival is finally packed and loaded onto the trucks. The sad and shabby caravan slowly pulls out from the muddy field onto the wet, deserted highway. In the last vehicle to pull away—a pickup truck—a skinny kid sits in the back. He is huddled, his back against the cab, under a thick, soiled tarp, close to sleep.

ACKNOWLEDGEMENTS

Iwould like to thank my dear friend and "first reader", Penny Beacham, for her critical comments and suggestions. A special thanks to Lisa England for her artistic contributions and technical assistance, and to Jennifer Nicholson for her suggestions and help with coordination in getting *Bad Creek* ready to print.